MODERN
EXPERIMENTAL
AIRCRAFT

Bruce LaFontaine

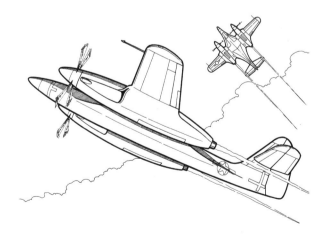

Dover Publications, Inc.
Mineola, New York

Bruce LaFontaine

Bruce LaFontaine is the illustrator and writer of more than thirty-one non-fiction children's books. His published works are sold in bookstores throughout the United States, Canada, and the United Kingdom. Mr. LaFontaine specializes in history, science, transportation, and architectural subjects for the children's middle-reader market (ages 8–12). He lives and works in the Rochester, New York area.

Illustration on Title Page: McDonnell XP-67 "BAT," 1944

Bibliographical Note

Modern Experimental Aircraft is a new work, first published by Dover Publications, Inc., in 2000.

DOVER *Pictorial Archive* SERIES

International Standard Book Number: 0-486-41037-4

Manufactured in the United States of America
Dover Publications, Inc., 31 East 2nd Street, Mineola, N.Y. 11501

INTRODUCTION

The years 1940 to 1990 represent the most exciting period in aviation history—when World War II, the immediate post-war era, and then the decades-long period of conflict between the United States and the Soviet Union known as the "Cold War," generated unprecedented advancements in airplane engineering and design. The aircraft depicted in this book derive from this fifty-year period exclusively.

No field of human endeavor drives technical progress as swiftly and eventfully as war, and World War II was no exception. The need for faster, bigger, and more deadly fighter and bomber aircraft threw aviation technology into fast forward mode. Economic and industrial resources were concentrated as never before into the effort to attain air superiority over the enemy. To this end, many types of experimental and prototype aircraft were developed in small numbers by the aviation industry to test new concepts, technologies, and materials. Some of the most successful were chosen for full-scale production and deployed into combat service by the thousands. Others were built only in limited quantities as test models for flight evaluation.

The successful use of the jet engine was the crowning achievement of World War II aviation. It was first utilized by the German Luftwaffe (Air Force) in the closing years of the war. Their jet-powered fighter plane, the Messerschmitt Me 262, was far more advanced than any of the Allied fighters of the day. Its twin turbojets slung under the wings could propel the Me 262 over 100 miles per hour faster than the best piston-engined propeller plane flown by the Allies. The viability of the jet engine, hastened by war needs, revolutionized aircraft design, both military and civilian.

In the post-war period, jet aircraft prototypes were numerous and varied. Some were hybrids, using both an old-style propeller engine and a turbojet for their propulsion. In those early days of jet engine technology, the engines themselves were both mechanically unreliable and extremely thirsty in their fuel consumption. Hence, the experimentation with models having a combination of engines. There are basically three types of jet engine. The early jet planes were powered by "turbojets," a device in which air is drawn into the engine inlet, compressed by spinning blades, ignited with fuel in a combustion chamber, and expelled out the back at high pressure with the aid of another set of turbine blades. The power of this exhaust pressure is measured in pounds of thrust. The first turbojet engines generated a fairly mild thrust of between 1,500 to 5,000 pounds. Modern "turbo*fan*" jet engines can produce 30,000 to 40,000 pounds of thrust each, since they use a larger set of compressor fan blades to deliver more thrust. Finally, an intermediate type of jet engine introduced in the 1950s is the "turboprop," which uses a turbojet to provide thrust, as well as to spin an externally mounted propeller. Turboprop engines, rated by horsepower rather than by pounds of thrust, can develop greater power than piston-driven propeller engines. A typical World War II propeller fighter could have an engine generating 1,500 to 2,100 horsepower, whereas post-war turboprop fighter prototypes described in this book had engines rated in the 5,000 to 6,000 horsepower range.

The undeclared "Cold War" between the United States and the Soviet Union, manifested chiefly by a fierce military arms race, began around 1948 and ended in 1989 with the economic collapse of the Soviet system. Each side devoted enormous resources to competing with the other in order to maintain a balance of power. With the United States economy in a post-war boom during the 1950s and 60s, aircraft companies and military planners worked hand in hand to develop new aviation technology through flying test models. In that era, it was still cost effective to explore new aircraft designs through relatively inexpensive prototypes that might cost a few hundred thousand dollars each. In today's economic climate, such experimental airplanes would cost millions—or even billions—to develop. In the last twenty-five years, the variety and number of experimental prototypes has declined dramatically from its height during the Cold War period.

In addition to making progress in jet-engine technology, aircraft prototypes have also been useful in developing improved construction materials and methods. High-strength stainless steel and titanium are now being incorporated into aircraft manufacture, as well as lightweight non-metallic "composite" materials such as plastic resins, kevlar, and carbon-fiber compounds. Advanced electronics and computers for faster, more efficient flight control systems have also been demonstrated by prototypes.

There are several categories of "X-Planes" described in this book. They are designated, with just a few exceptions, by the "X" or the "Y" prefix. An "X" designation signals the first of one or several experimental aircraft, while the "Y" designation denotes a follow-up model—usually versions that are improved by data gathered from the test flights of the initial "X" model(s). Some of the first entries in this book are identified as "XP" models, which indicates an "Experimental Pursuit" aircraft. Pursuit plane was the early name given to what are now called Fighters. The Air Force changed the prefix "P" for Pursuit to "F" for Fighter in 1948, which is why a transitional aircraft like the Lockheed "Shooting Star" is labelled both a P-80 (from 1946 to 1948), and an F-80 (1948 onward). Other entries in this book are more straightforward, and are designated "XB" or "YB," representing an Experimental Bomber prototype. A third class of X-Plane is the pure research aircraft, not intended as predecessor to any production airplane, but solely as a test-bed for new technology. These X-Planes were flown and tested at Edwards Air Force Base Flight Test Center in the California desert. Examples of this kind of dedicated research airplane are the Bell X-1, X-2, and X-5, the Douglas X-3, the Northrop X-4, and the North American X-15.

In the remarkable fifty-year period of aeronautics covered in this book, aircraft have advanced from top speeds of 400 miles per hour to over 4,000 miles per hour. At this rate of progress, one can only imagine the magnitude of the next exciting leap in aviation achievement.

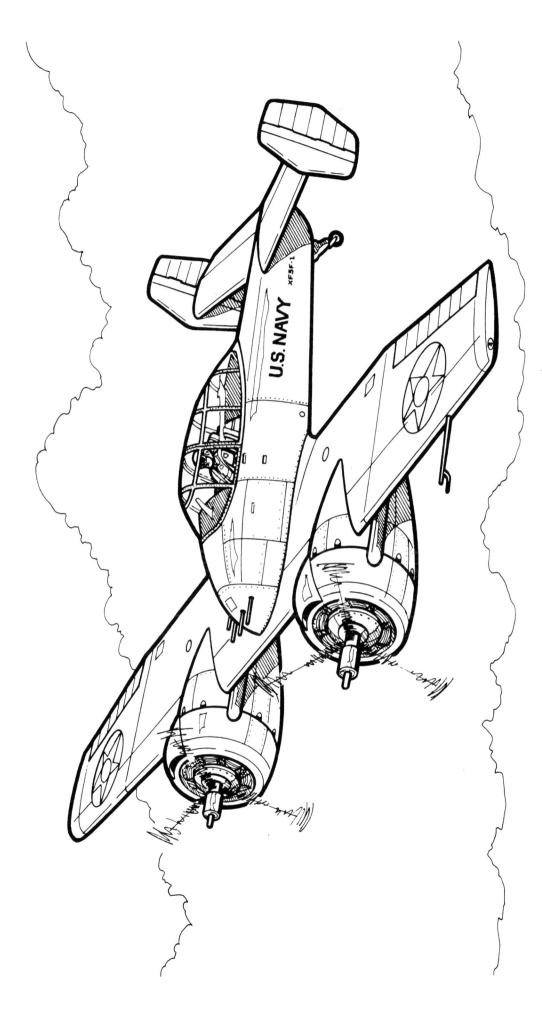

GRUMMAN XF5F-1 "SKYROCKET," 1940

Before the United States entered World War II in December of 1941, Grumman Aircraft built and conducted test flights with the radical-looking XF5F-1 "Skyrocket" fighter for the U.S. Navy, which was interested in developing a fast, maneuverable twin-engine fighter for its growing fleet of aircraft carriers. The XF5F-1 was equipped with two 1,200-horsepower Wright radial engines spinning three-bladed propellers. The fuselage was mounted at the forward leading edge of the wing, providing excellent pilot vision and maneuverability. It had a very fast top speed of 383 miles per hour, and was intended to be armed with can-

non and machine guns. The plane served as a valuable prototype for the Navy's later operational twin-engine propeller fighter, the F7F Tigercat, deployed with the fleet in 1946.

The Skyrocket was painted in the Navy's pre-World War II color scheme of silver fuselage and engine nacelles (housings), bright yellow wings, and tail rudders with one vertical blue stripe preceding red-and-white horizontal stripes. The U.S. national insignia at this time was a large blue circle—called a "roundel"—enclosing a white star with a smaller red circle at its center.

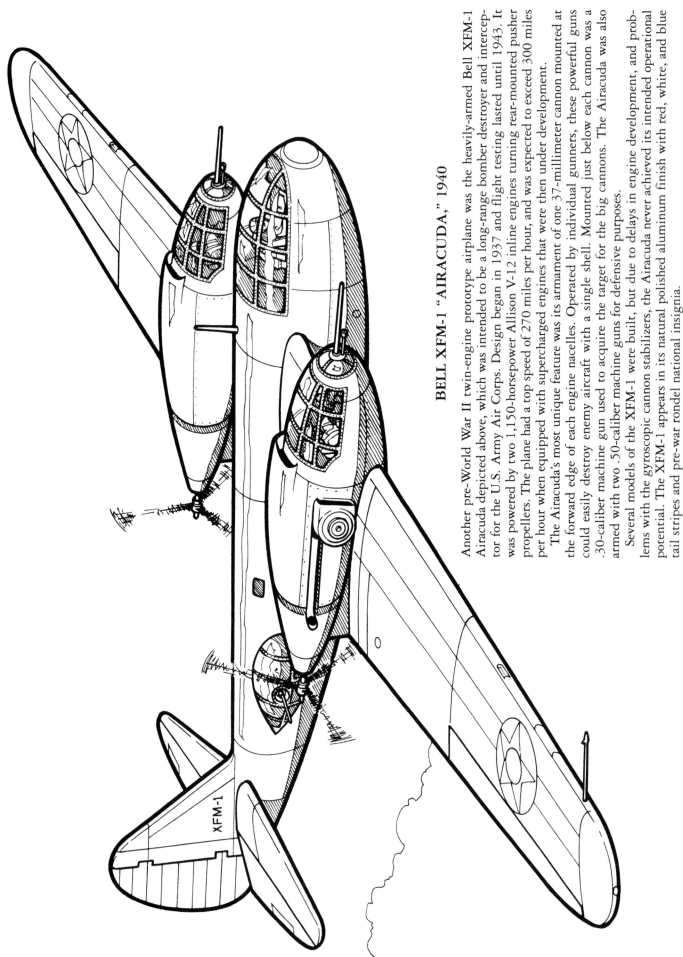

BELL XFM-1 "AIRACUDA," 1940

Another pre-World War II twin-engine prototype airplane was the heavily-armed Bell XFM-1 Airacuda depicted above, which was intended to be a long-range bomber destroyer and interceptor for the U.S. Army Air Corps. Design began in 1937 and flight testing lasted until 1943. It was powered by two 1,150-horsepower Allison V-12 inline engines turning rear-mounted pusher propellers. The plane had a top speed of 270 miles per hour, and was expected to exceed 300 miles per hour when equipped with supercharged engines that were then under development.

The Airacuda's most unique feature was its armament of one 37-millimeter cannon mounted at the forward edge of each engine nacelles. Operated by individual gunners, these powerful guns could easily destroy enemy aircraft with a single shell. Mounted just below each cannon was a .30-caliber machine gun used to acquire the target for the big cannons. The Airacuda was also armed with two .50-caliber machine guns for defensive purposes.

Several models of the XFM-1 were built, but due to delays in engine development, and problems with the gyroscopic cannon stabilizers, the Airacuda never achieved its intended operational potential. The XFM-1 appears in its natural polished aluminum finish with red, white, and blue tail stripes and pre-war rondel national insignia.

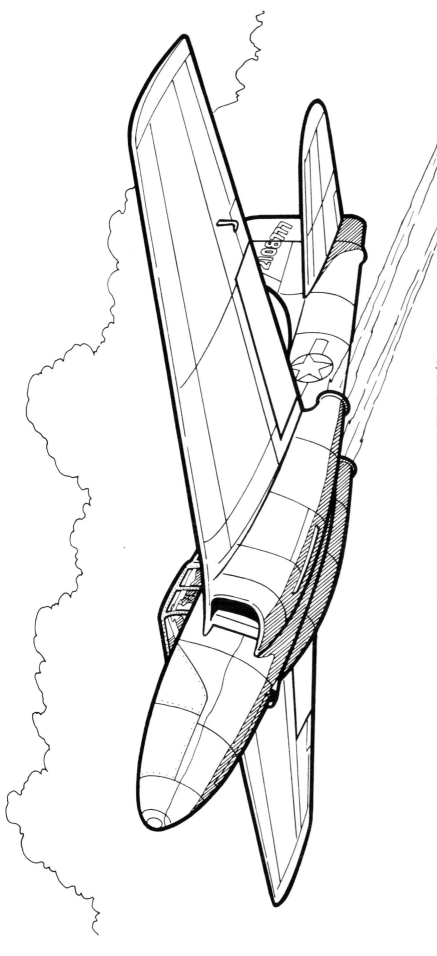

BELL XP-59 "AIRACOMET," 1942

Bell Aircraft of Buffalo, New York was instrumental in developing many of the advanced experimental and prototype aircraft of the 1940s and 1950s. In 1942, they made a successful test flight with the first American jet aircraft, the XP-59 Airacomet fighter.

Jet aircraft were initially designed and built by the German Air Force during World War II. They deployed the first operational combat jet fighter, the highly advanced Messerschmitt Me 262, in 1943. This aircraft was powered by two jet engines and could reach a speed of 540 miles per hour, 100 miles per hour faster than the best Allied fighters of the era. In order to challenge this radical leap forward in fighter technology and performance, the British and Americans began intensive development of their own jet aircraft.

The first British jet fighter, the Gloster Meteor Mark I, became operational in 1944. It was powered by two Rolls Royce turbojet engines. The American effort, the Bell XP-59, used engines based on these British power plants. A number of models of the XP-59 and follow-up YP-59 were built and flown from 1943 to 1945. However, the Airacomet's performance was disappointing; and with a maximum speed of only 413 miles per hour, the aircraft never went into widespread production or operational service. It did, however, serve as a valuable instrument for future American jet fighter development. Data gathered by flight testing of the XP-59 led to the introduction of the first operational American jet fighter—the Lockheed P/F-80 "Shooting Star" in 1945.

The Airacomets that were test flown either remained in their natural polished metal finish, or painted in standard U.S. Army Air Corps World War II camouflage colors of olive drab fuselage and wing top surfaces, with light gray undersurfaces. By the beginning of World War II, America's national insignia had changed to a blue rondel enclosing a white star, flanked by two white bars on either side.

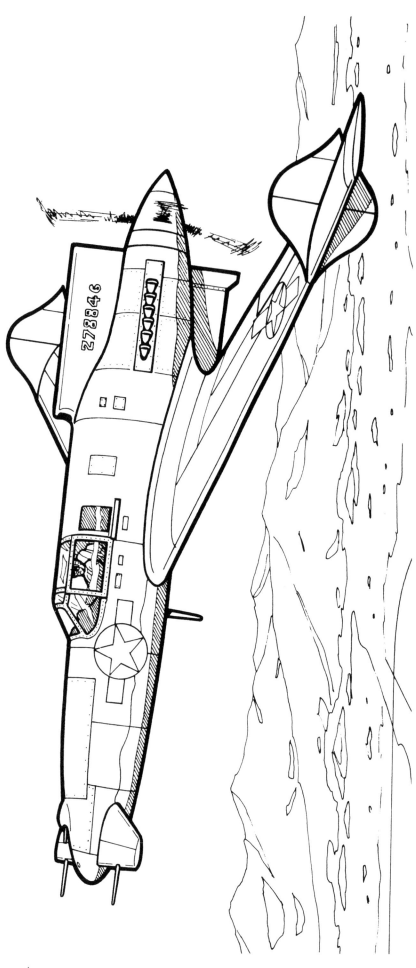

CURTISS XP-55 "ASCENDER," 1943

Glenn Curtiss was a contemporary of the Wright Brothers in the early pioneering days of aviation. Curtiss began building and flying pontoon-equipped biplanes on Kueka Lake, near Hammondsport, New York in 1911. From this simple beginning, Curtiss Aircraft—a giant in the history of aviation—was born.

During the years 1911–1939, Curtiss Aircraft designed and built numerous highly successful fighters, bombers, floatplanes, and transports for both the U.S. Navy and Army Air Corps. In 1940, the Air Corps initiated a design competition for an advanced fighter plane. Competing for this contract were three of the premier aircraft companies of the day: Northrop with their XP-56 "Black Bullet," Consolidated Vultee with their XP-54 "Swoose Goose," and Curtiss with their unusual-looking XP-55 Ascender shown above.

The XP-55 incorporated the radical concept of swept-back wings to lower drag and increase speed, and forward-mounted mini-wings called "canards" for increased lift and maneuverability. Instead of a conventional vertical fin and rudder rising from the rear of the aircraft, the Ascender was equipped with wing tip-mounted vertical fins for directional stability and control. The XP-55 was powered by a rear-mounted Allison V-12 propeller engine rated at 1,275 horsepower. With this power plant, the Ascender could reach a respectable top speed of 390 miles per hour. A newer, more powerful Allison engine of 2,200 horsepower was under development, but was never installed in the XP-55. It would have given the aircraft a record top speed of 500 miles per hour.

Of the three prototypes built for flight testing, one crashed in 1943, while the other two continued in the evaluation against the competitors from Northrop and Consolidated Vultee. Because of directional control problems caused by its radical airframe design, the XP-55 did not prove stable enough for full operational production. Eventually, all of the competing aircraft programs in the 1940 Air Corps advanced fighter design contest were cancelled in favor of wartime production of more conventional existing fighters. The XP-55 models were painted in the standard early World War II Army Air Corps camouflage colors of olive drab top surfaces and light gray undersurfaces.

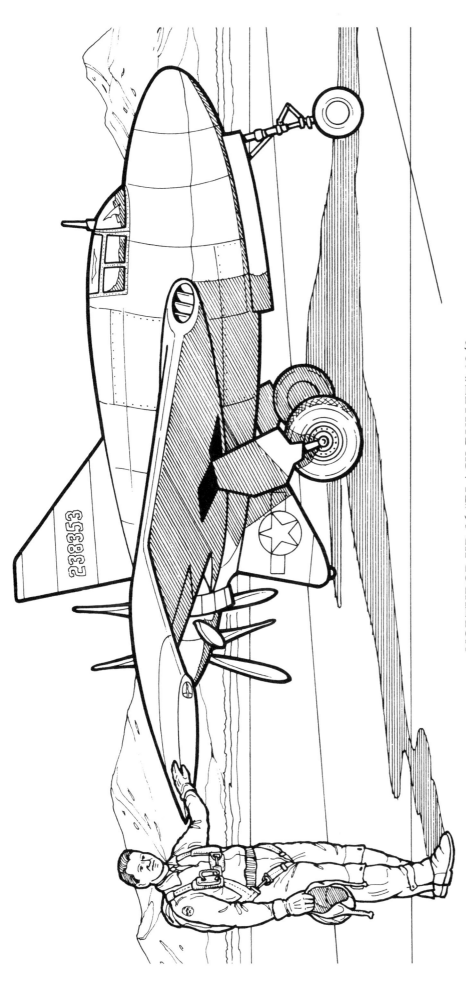

NORTHROP XP-56 "BLACK BULLET," 1943

Jack Northrop was among the most innovative of the great aircraft designers of the 1930s and 40s. His primary focus in his advanced airplane prototypes was on the concept of the "flying wing." This unique idea blended the fuselage and wing into one continuous streamlined airframe which, in theory, meant less drag to increase speed and provide tremendous lift from the continuous large wing airfoil. In this period, Northrop produced a number of flying-wing models with varying degrees of success.

Shown above is the XP-56, nicknamed the Black Bullet, Northrop's entry into the 1940 Air Corps design competition for an advanced fighter. It was built with an all-welded magnesium airframe, a radical construction method for the era. Magnesium is a durable, strong, yet very lightweight metal. It was driven by a 2,000-horsepower Pratt & Whitney R-2800 radial engine mounted in the rear. This formidable power plant turned two sets of three-bladed propellers spinning

in opposite directions—called "contra-rotating"—to provide greater forward thrust and speed. The Black Bullet incorporated a large swept-back wing with its fairly small fuselage size in an attempt at a modified flying-wing design. With its powerful engine and light weight, the XP-56 was able to attain a top speed of 465 miles per hour, very fast for its time. Again, like its Curtiss competitor—the XP-55—the XP-56 suffered from stability and control problems due to the unusual overall design, and was never approved for production.

Two prototypes were built for evaluation, with flight testing beginning in 1943. The first version had small stubby vertical fins mounted on the top and bottom of the tail, and was flown in its natural magnesium finish. The second model—depicted above—had the vertical fins increased in size to provide greater stability. This model was painted in standard Air Corps olive drab and gray

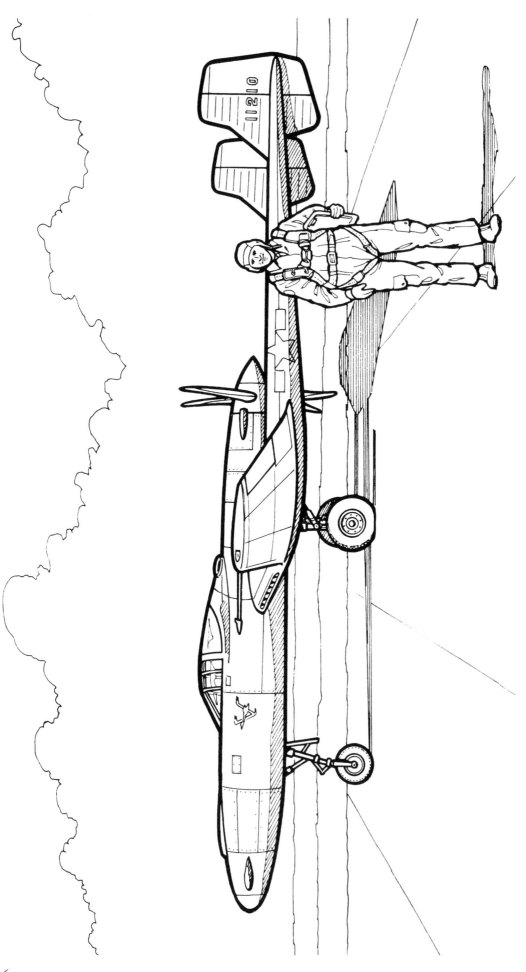

CONSOLIDATED VULTEE XP-54 "SWOOSE GOOSE," 1943

The third entry in the advanced fighter design competition was the Consolidated Vultee Aircraft Company XP-54 Swoose Goose—not to be confused with the World War II B-17 bomber with the same nickname. This prototype also featured a rear-mounted engine driving a single pusher propeller. The engine was located at the back of a short bullet-like fuselage situated between two tail booms projecting back from the conventional straight wings. The power plant was an unusual Lycoming XH-2470 liquid-cooled engine comprised of four banks of six cylinders. Large and heavy, this engine produced a formidable 2,300 horsepower.

Another singular feature of the XP-54 was a swivelling gun arrangement mounted in the nose. This complex system would allow the six .50-caliber machine guns to rotate up and down to increase their firing area. Problems with this mechanism and a relatively slow top speed of 380 miles per hour effectively ended the development of the XP-54.

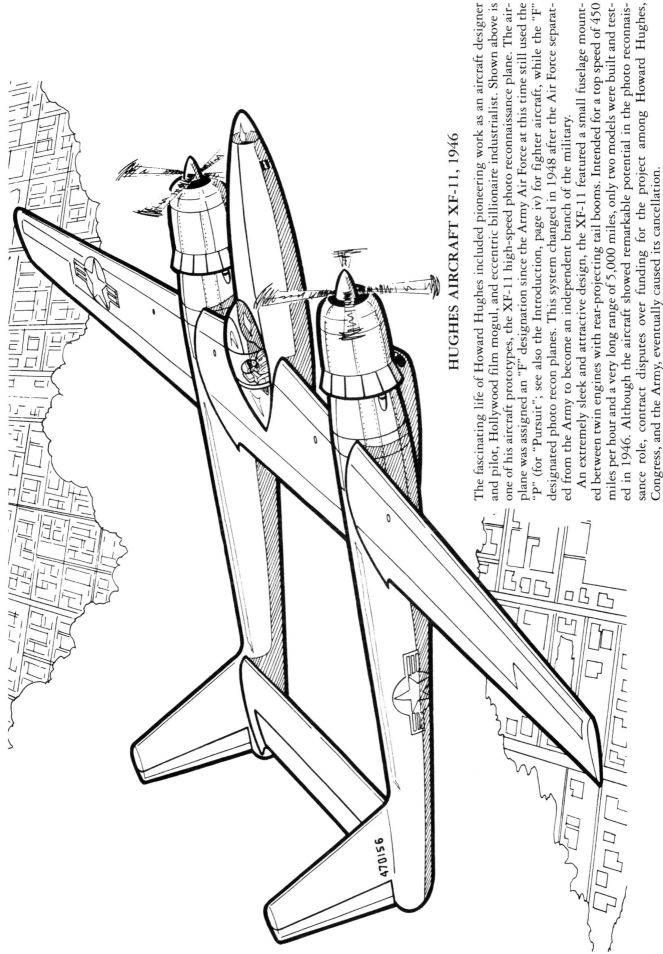

HUGHES AIRCRAFT XF-11, 1946

The fascinating life of Howard Hughes included pioneering work as an aircraft designer and pilot, Hollywood film mogul, and eccentric billionaire industrialist. Shown above is one of his aircraft prototypes, the XF-11 high-speed photo reconnaissance plane. The airplane was assigned an "F" designation since the Army Air Force at this time still used the "P" (for "Pursuit"; see also the Introduction, page iv) for fighter aircraft, while the "F" designated photo recon planes. This system changed in 1948 after the Air Force separated from the Army to become an independent branch of the military.

An extremely sleek and attractive design, the XF-11 featured a small fuselage mounted between twin engines with rear-projecting tail booms. Intended for a top speed of 450 miles per hour and a very long range of 5,000 miles, only two models were built and tested in 1946. Although the aircraft showed remarkable potential in the photo reconnaissance role, contract disputes over funding for the project among Howard Hughes, Congress, and the Army, eventually caused its cancellation.

Clarence "Kelly" Johnson

LOCKHEED YP-80A "SHOOTING STAR," 1944

Throughout the five years that spanned the Second World War (1939–1945), there was a tremendous acceleration in the advancement of aircraft design and engine technology. Driven by the demands of warfare for superior combat planes, the United States, Great Britain, and Germany achieved major breakthroughs in aviation. First and foremost among these developments was the jet-engined aircraft. The speed and overall performance of these new airplanes made the best of the piston-engined, propeller-driven fighters of that era obsolete within a few short years.

By 1945, all three major combatants had jet-fighter aircraft. The first was the fast and deadly German Messerschmitt Me 262, soon followed by the slower but still effective British Gloster Meteor Mark I. Both of these planes saw combat service during the war, although never in air-to-air battles. Lastly, the first American jet fighter to go into operational service—the Lockheed P-80 Shooting Star—was introduced. A squadron of P-80s was actually posted to Italy in 1945 before the end of the war, but they were flown solely for training and not for combat missions.

The initial model of the P-80—the XP-80 "LuLu Belle"—was first flown in 1944 over Muroc Dry Lake, California, home of the Army Air Force Flight Test Center. A number of additional XP-80s were built and flown, followed by faster and improved YP-80 proto-

types. The first 1,000 production model P-80A's were ordered by the Army Air Force in 1945. These fighters were fast and maneuverable with a top speed of 550 miles per hour. The final version of the Shooting Star—the P-80C—had a top speed of 580 miles per hour, and was used extensively and effectively as a fighter-bomber during the Korean War (1950–1953). In 1948, the Air Force became a separate military service from the Army, and changed the designation for its fighter planes from "P" (for "Pursuit") to the current designation, "F" (for "Fighter"), which is why the Shooting Star is referred to as both the P-80 and F-80.

Pictured above with the YP-80A is the designer of the aircraft, Clarence "Kelly" Johnson, who is considered the most talented and prolific airplane engineer in the history of aviation. At Lockheed—mostly at their top secret advanced aircraft development facility nicknamed the "Skunk Works"—Kelly Johnson supervised the creation of a remarkable number of historic aircraft. Under his guidance, Lockheed built the World War II twin-engine fighter, the P-38 "Lightning"; the P/F-80; the U-2 high altitude spyplane; the supersonic F-104 "Starfighter"; the fastest and highest flying aircraft still in service, the SR-71 "Blackbird" spyplane; and started work on the radar-evading stealth aircraft, the F-117A "Nighthawk." Kelly Johnson died in 1990 after a distinguished 45-year career in aviation.

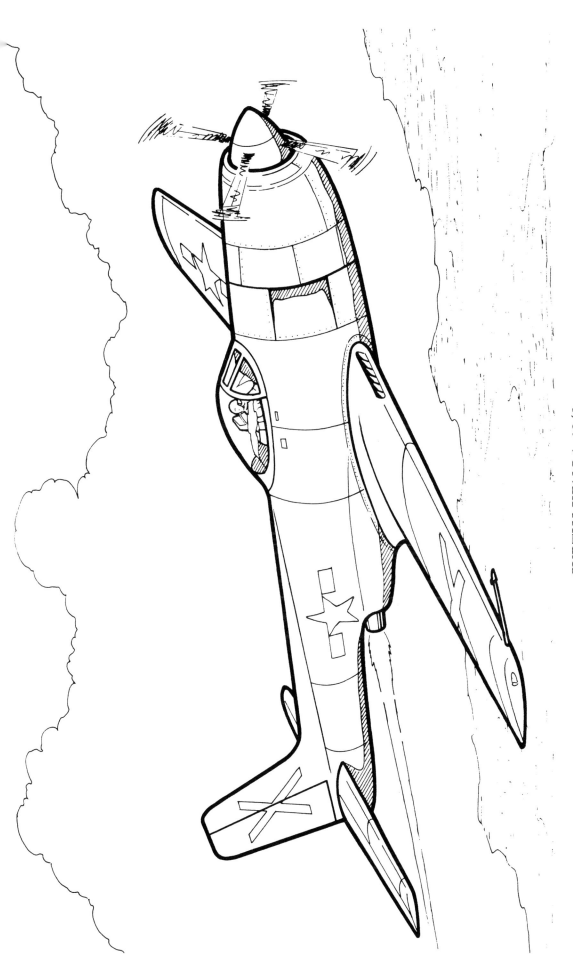

CURTISS XF15C-1, 1945

Early jet aircraft, although much faster than their propeller-driven counterparts, were prone to both excessive fuel usage and mechanical breakdowns. In the propeller-to-jet aircraft transition years of the late 1940s, both the Navy and Air Force issued contracts to numerous aircraft builders for hybrids—planes that were equipped with both types of engines. Shown above is one of these combination fighters developed for the Navy by Curtiss Aircraft. The XF15C-1 was first flown in 1945 using its 2,100-horsepower radial-propeller engine, and a turbojet engine providing 2,700 pounds of thrust out of the rear jet exhaust pipe. It was able to attain a speed of 469 miles per hour, not much faster than the best piston-engined Navy fighter of the day, the Grumman F8F "Bearcat." As jet engine technology became more reliable and efficient, the military lost interest in these hybrid fighters in favor of pure jets.

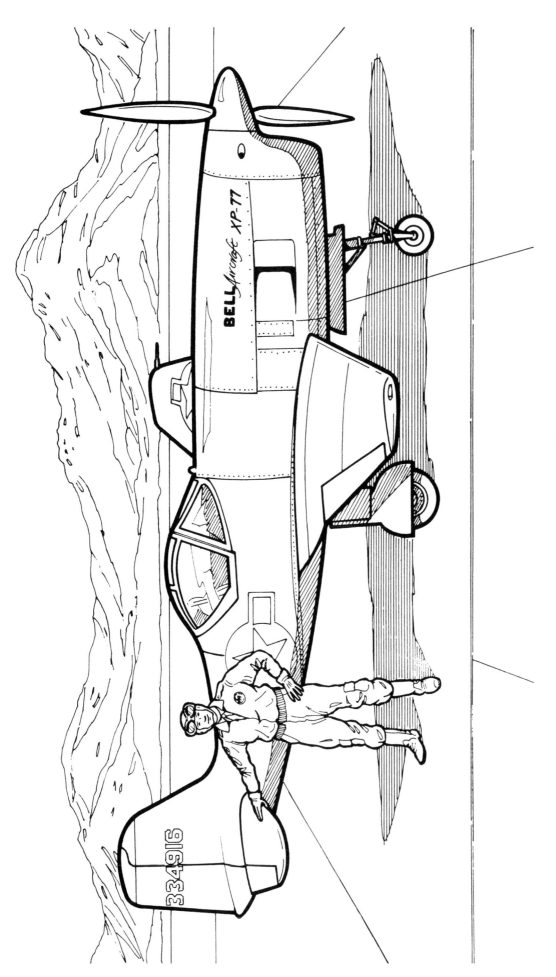

BELL XP-77, 1944

Bell Aircraft developed a prototype for a small, lightweight fighter, the XP-77, that could be easily and cheaply produced using a bare minimum of strategic war materials like aluminum. First flown in 1944, the XP-77 was constructed mainly from wood, and was powered by a 670-horsepower piston engine driving a two-bladed propeller. It was twenty-three feet long, ten-feet high at the tail, and had a wingspan of just twenty-seven feet. With its intended armament of two .50-caliber fuselage-mounted machine guns, the XP-77 weighed only 3,500 pounds fully fueled. Its relatively small engine could propel the wooden fighter to a speed of 330 miles per hour. Only two XP-77 models were built and tested. And since the war was drawing to a close at this time, there was no further development of this diminutive fighter. The project was officially cancelled in 1945.

CONSOLIDATED VULTEE XP-81, 1945

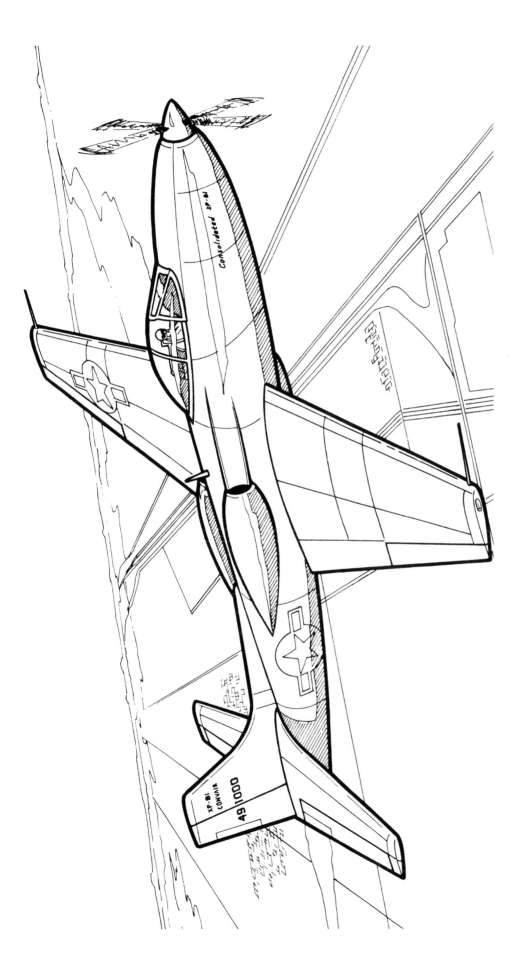

By the end of World War II, aircraft engine manufacturers had in development another new type of power plant, the turboprop engine. A mix of jet technology and propeller thrust, the turboprop showed great potential for generating much higher levels of horsepower than piston-engined propeller types. A turboprop is basically a gasoline engine using combustion to turn an internal turbine wheel. This spinning motion, along with the engine's hot exhaust gases, is used to turn a drive shaft connected to a conventional outside-mounted propeller.

Pictured above is a long range fighter-interceptor prototype developed by Consolidated Vultee Aircraft using the combination of a turboprop and a pure turbojet engine. The XP-81 was developed in 1944, and first flew in 1945. Technical difficulties with the engine delayed installation of the 2,300-horse-

power General Electric TG-100 turboprop, so the XP-81's initial test flights were flown with a conventional Merlin piston engine driving the nose-mounted propeller. A mid-mounted Allison J-33 turbojet engine supplied 3,750 pounds of thrust from the rear jet exhaust pipe. The air intakes for the jet engine can be clearly seen on the top of the fuselage behind the bubble canopy. The XP-81 was flown in its natural polished metal finish.

Subsequent flights were made with the more powerful turboprop engine, and the aircraft performed at an impressive top speed of 490 miles per hour. Despite its high speed and good flight-handling characteristics, the XP-81 suffered the same fate as many of the other experimental aircraft prototypes developed during World War II, and the project was cancelled shortly after the war ended.

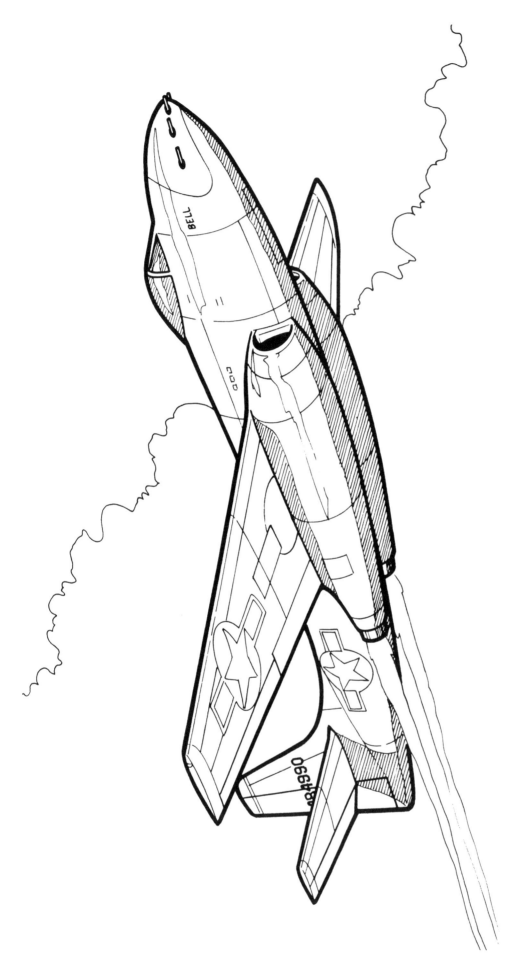

BELL XP-83, 1945

Designed to be a speedier successor to the XP-59, Bell Aircraft developed and flew the XP-83 starting in 1945. It was intended as a long range single-seat fighter-interceptor with an armament of six nose-mounted .50-caliber machine guns. The plane was powered by two General Electric J-33 turbojets producing 4,000 pounds of thrust apiece. A large and heavy aircraft, the XP-83 was able to reach a top speed of just over 500 miles per hour—a performance that did not warrant continued development—so the project was cancelled in 1946.

Although the XP-83 was the final fighter design created by Bell Aircraft, the company shifted its efforts into producing a series of extremely successful experimental research aircraft intended to explore the limits of high-speed flight. Powered by both jet and rocket engines, Bell's X-Planes of the late 40s and early 50s were among the most important experimental aircraft ever flown. The two XP-83 flying prototypes were left in their natural aluminum color.

NORTHROP XP-79, 1945

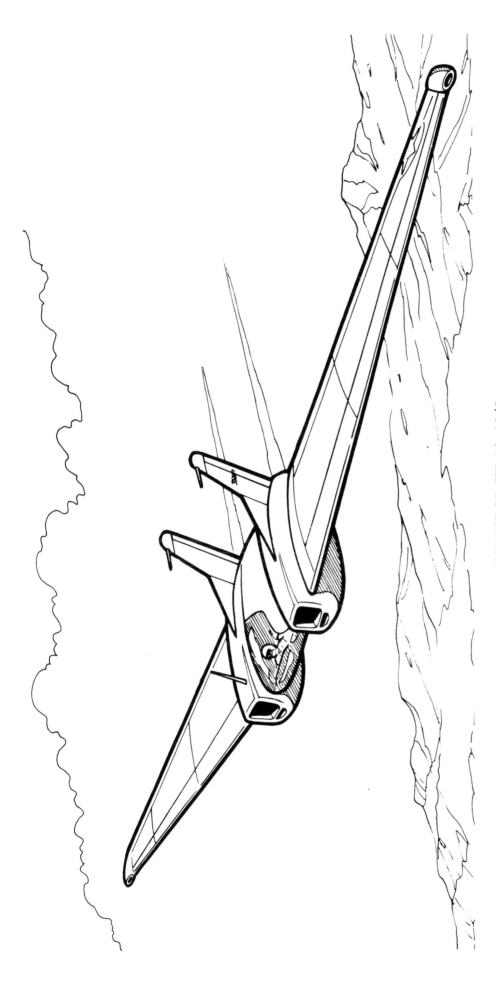

Jack Northrop's flying-wing aircraft concept was realized with the construction of the XP-79 fighter-interceptor pictured above. Its overall configuration was based on the earlier Northrop N9-M propeller-driven flying-wing prototype of 1942. The XP-79 was originally conceived to be rocket-propelled, but was redesigned to incorporate two Westinghouse 19B turbojets, each providing 1,365 pounds of thrust. It was projected to have a top speed of 550 miles per hour.

The XP-79 was fabricated from welded magnesium, a very unusual aircraft construction method. It also featured specially reinforced wing leading edges intended to enable the XP-79 to ram and slice the tails of enemy bombers. Additional armament planned were four .50-caliber machine guns for more conventional aerial combat. The wing tips featured air scoops to provide pneumati-

cally-assisted control of the wing ailerons and elevons (control flaps). For flight testing purposes, the XP-79 was painted bright yellow to make it more visible to ground-based observers.

Perhaps the most radical feature of the XP-79 was the pilot's flight position. He was situated at the very forward edge of the Plexiglas™ canopy lying in a prone (horizontal) position. A special chin-and-head support allowed him to look forward to control his flight. This awkward flying position was not well received by potential test pilots. The XP-79's sole test flight took place on September 12, 1945. During testing, electrical problems caused a loss of control and the plane went into a fatal spin. Northrop test pilot Harry Crosby was killed in the crash. The XP-79 project was cancelled in 1946.

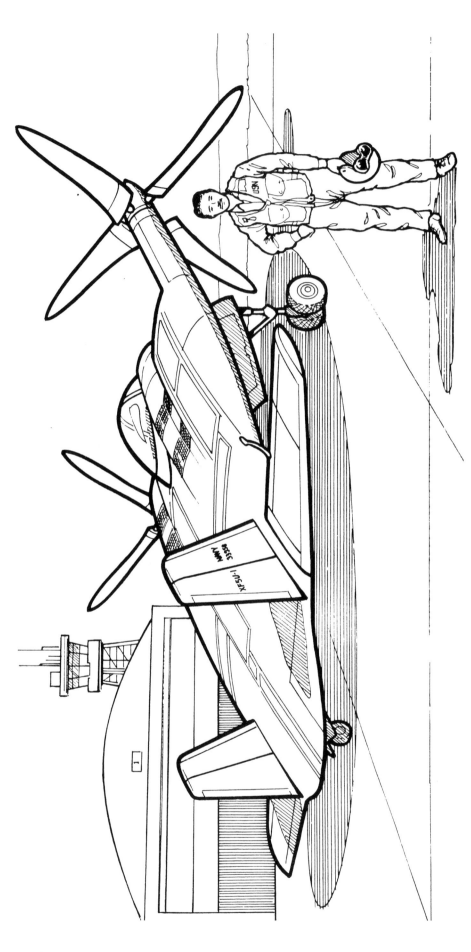

VOUGHT XF5U-1 SKIMMER "FLYING PANCAKE," 1947

Perhaps the oddest looking experimental aircraft prototype ever built was the Vought XF5U-1, depicted above. It had virtually no wings. Its aerodynamic lift was to be provided by the airflow from its huge sixteen-foot long propellers passing over its circular lifting-body fuselage. In 1944, Vought aircraft received a contract from the U.S. Navy to implement this concept for a carrier-based fighter plane. The unusual shape of the Flying Pancake was intended to allow it to land at slow speed on aircraft carriers with short take-off and landing capabilities.

The single XF5U-1 aircraft was based on an earlier Vought flying prototype, the V-173. Test flown for the Navy in 1942, this initial model featured much less powerful engines than the proposed production version of the XF5U-1, but was quite successful at low-speed landings. The Navy ordered two models of the XF5U-1 in 1944. These were to be powered by two turbo-supercharged Pratt & Whitney R-2000 engines developing 1,400 horsepower each. Another unusual aspect of the XF5U-1 was the construction material of its airframe, which was fabricated from "metalite"—a composite material made from a sheet of balsa wood sandwiched between two sheets of aluminum. This provided a very strong but lightweight skin for the aircraft. The Flying Pancake was painted in the standard Navy post-war color scheme of overall dark sea blue.

Development problems with the unusual wide-bladed propellers delayed final construction until 1947. By the time the XF5U-1 prototype was ready for testing, the Navy had already lost interest in the project, preferring to turn their attention to the development of jet-fighter aircraft. The single XF5U-1 prototype was never test flown, and it was scrapped in 1948.

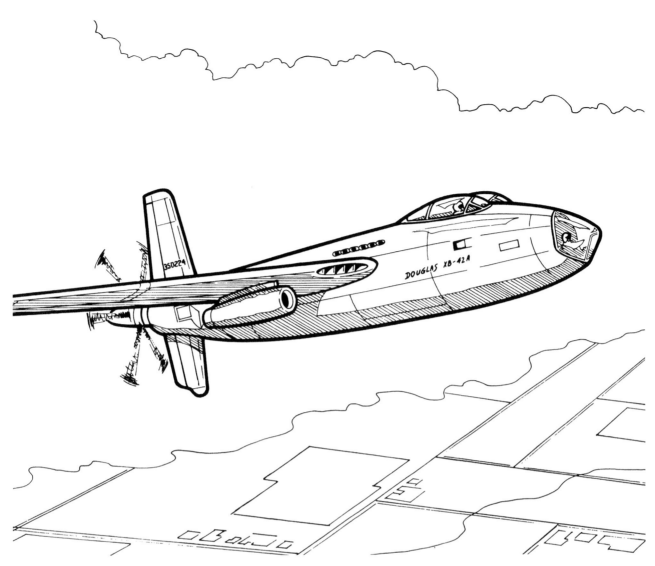

DOUGLAS XB-42A, 1947

Douglas Aircraft had made a long and noteworthy contribution to aviation history, most notably with their DC-3/C-47 airliner and cargo transport airplane, first flown in 1936. The DC-3 airliner version was the virtual foundation for the modern air transport industry. With over 12,000 built since 1936, many are still in service with smaller airlines throughout the world. Douglas also developed several important bomber aircraft during World War II. In the early war years, their A-20 "Havoc" medium bomber (also called an "attack plane") was used extensively by the United States and its allies. Toward the end of the war, Douglas introduced the B-26 "Invader" (later designated A-26), which many aviation experts regard as the finest medium bomber of the war. It was very fast, heavily armed, and ruggedly built.

As jet technology was beginning to emerge in the late war years, the Army Air Force issued contracts to several aircraft companies to develop a medium bomber with high speed and long-range capabilities. The first Douglas prototype for this type of bomber was the XB-42, nicknamed the "Mixmaster," an allusion to its dual counter-rotating rear pusher propellers. Although the first model was not jet-powered, the basic airframe was designed to be converted to jet power when engine technology became more advanced. For its initial test flights

in 1944, the XB-42 was powered by two supercharged Allison inline piston engines, each rated at 1,900 horsepower, and mounted side-by-side within the rear fuselage. These engines turned dual three-bladed counter-rotating propellers. With its very clean, aerodynamic airframe, the XB-42 had a top speed of 386 miles per hour, very fast for a bomber of this era. The pilot and copilot sat in an unusual side-by-side position, each under their own "bug-eye" Plexiglas™ canopy.

The second prototype, the XB-42A pictured above, was ready for flight testing in 1947. This version had the additional power of two Westinghouse XJ-30 turbojet engines mounted under the wings, which provided an additional 1,600 pounds of thrust apiece. With this combination of jet propulsion and its 3,800-horsepower propeller engines, the XB-42A could reach a speed of 473 miles per hour. The final version of this aircraft, redesignated the XB-43, was a pure jet-engined prototype, powered by two General Electric J-35 turbojets rated at 3,820 pounds of thrust each. It had a top speed of 507 miles per hour. Although the XB-42 and XB-43 series of prototypes never went into full-scale production, they provided valuable test-flight data for the next generation of jet bombers that were deployed into operational service by 1950.

NORTHROP XB-35 "FLYING WING," 1946

The ultimate culmination of Jack Northrop's radical "flying wing" concept was the intercontinental heavy bomber prototype: the XB-35, and its jet-powered successor, the YB-49. Both aircraft used the same overall design and huge all-wing airframe. The XB-35 was developed as a top-secret project during World War II, designed to carry a 10,000-pound bomb-load at high speed from bases in the United States to Berlin and back.

The XB-35 was powered by four massive Pratt & Whitney 3,000-horsepower piston engines buried deep in the wing itself. Large air scoops mounted at the wing leading edges provided cooling air for these mighty power plants. Through a complex system of gearboxes and driveshafts, each engine drove a pair of counter-rotating four-bladed propellers. Top speed was estimated at 400 miles per hour. The XB-35 was well equipped with defensive armament, featuring turrets with twin .50-caliber machine guns mounted on outboard wing positions on both the top and bottom wing surfaces, as well as a central top-mounted four-gun turret and four-gun tail-cone emplacement. A gunner remotely controlled the guns from a central observation blister behind the pilot's Plexiglas™ canopy.

The first two prototypes of the XB-35 were tested over Muroc Dry Lake Flight Test Center in 1946. Continuing problems with the complex engine and transmission mechanisms associated with the counter-rotating propellers prevented the XB-35's from achieving their intended speed and range potential. The piston-engined XB-35 project was cancelled by the Air Force in favor of the more conventional and larger B-36 intercontinental bomber. However, the existing airframes were maintained and eventually redesigned to incorporate jet engines in a new long-range bomber, the YB-49. Both the XB-35 and YB-49 prototypes were flown in their natural silver finish.

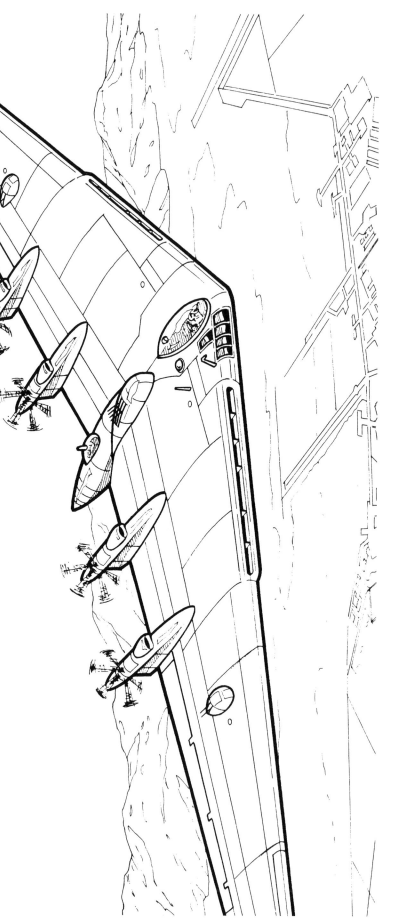

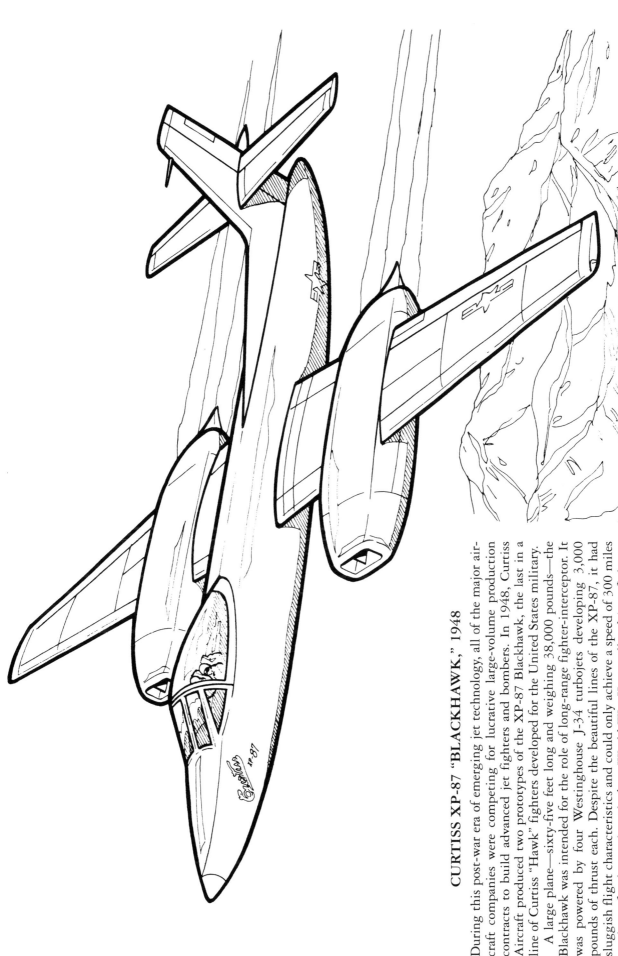

CURTISS XP-87 "BLACKHAWK," 1948

During this post-war era of emerging jet technology, all of the major aircraft companies were competing for lucrative large-volume production contracts to build advanced jet fighters and bombers. In 1948, Curtiss Aircraft produced two prototypes of the XP-87 Blackhawk, the last in a line of Curtiss "Hawk" fighters developed for the United States military.

A large plane—sixty-five feet long and weighing 38,000 pounds—the Blackhawk was intended for the role of long-range fighter-interceptor. It was powered by four Westinghouse J-34 turbojets developing 3,000 pounds of thrust each. Despite the beautiful lines of the XP-87, it had sluggish flight characteristics and could only achieve a speed of 300 miles per hour, far slower than the best World War II propeller-driven fighters. After test flight evaluation, the Air Force chose the rival Northrop XP-89 for its long-range interceptor production model. The Blackhawk—as the name implies—was painted in a high-gloss jet black color scheme.

17

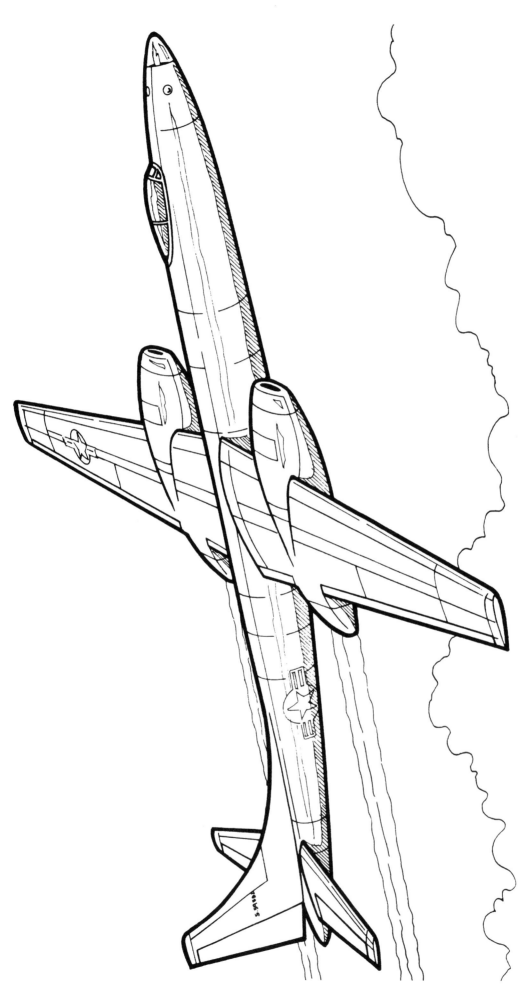

CONVAIR XB-46, 1947

In an effort to compete with other companies for a contract to build an advanced medium jet bomber, Consolidated Vultee Aircraft—which had hitherto been two separate companies—merged to become Convair, one of the most successful builders of high-speed jet fighters and bombers of the 1950s and 60s. Pictured above is their 1947 design for a four jet-engined medium bomber, the XP-46. Despite its extremely clean and elegant aerodynamics, this prototype was able to reach a disappointing speed of just 490 miles per hour. It was powered by four Allison J-35 turbojets mounted in pairs under each wing. Each engine developed 4,000 pounds of thrust, not enough power for this large and heavy aircraft. The lighter and faster North American XB-45 "Tornado" won out over the XB-46 in the medium bomber contract competition.

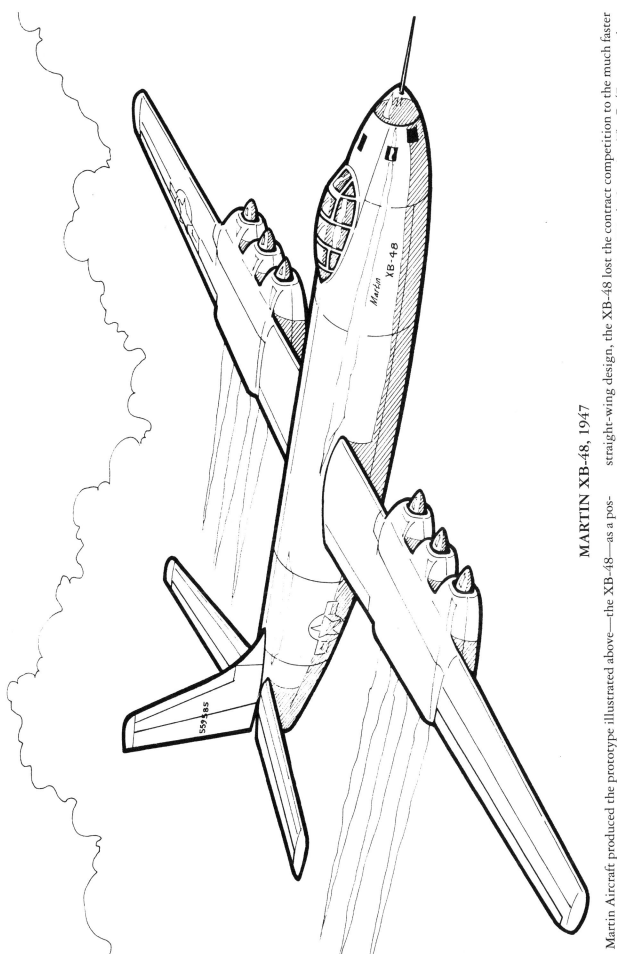

MARTIN XB-48, 1947

Martin Aircraft produced the prototype illustrated above—the XB-48—as a possible contender for the medium jet bomber market. It was powered by six turbojet engines, mounted in threes under each wing. Despite this increase in the number of engines, the XB-48 was only twenty miles per hour faster than the four-engined XB-46. With its rather ungainly looking and conventional straight-wing design, the XB-48 lost the contract competition to the much faster and more advanced swept-wing Boeing XB-47 Stratojet. The B-47 was put into full-scale production, and was a mainstay of the Strategic Air Command's bomber fleet for many years.

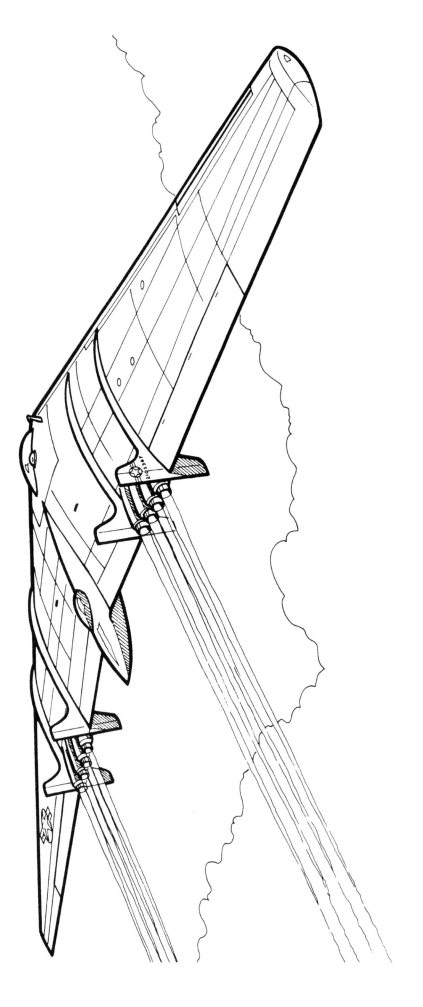

NORTHROP YB-49 "FLYING WING," 1947

Three Northrop XB-35 prototypes were converted to YB-49 models in 1947. The troublesome counter-rotating propeller piston engines were replaced by eight turbojets. These Allison J-35 jet engines each produced 4,000 pounds of thrust, giving the YB-49 an increase in speed to a maximum of 490 miles per hour—100 miles per hour faster than the piston-engined XB-35. Additionally, four vertical fins were added to the wing trailing edge to increase directional stability.

Test pilots reported that the big YB-49 flew well, handling more like a fighter than a 193,000-pound intercontinental bomber. Unfortunately, during flight evaluation over Muroc Dry Lake testing center, both flying-wing prototypes crashed and were destroyed. Chief test pilot Captain Glenn Edwards—killed in

the crash—was memorialized by Muroc Dry Lake Flight Test Center being renamed in his honor. Edwards Air Force Base became famous as the location for the test flights of many famous, record-breaking experimental aircraft.

With the destruction of the YB-49 prototypes, Jack Northrop's dream of large flying-wing aircraft ended. Ironically, about three decades later, Northrop Aircraft would become the builder of the top secret, radar-evading B-2 "Spirit" stealth bomber. The B-2, begun in the 1980s and revealed to the public in the 1990s, is a flying-wing design with the exact 172-foot wingspan of Northrop's original XB-35 and YB-49. As a tribute to his pioneering work in aircraft design, special security arrangements were made to allow Jack Northrop to see the B-2's engineering plans shortly before his death in 1981.

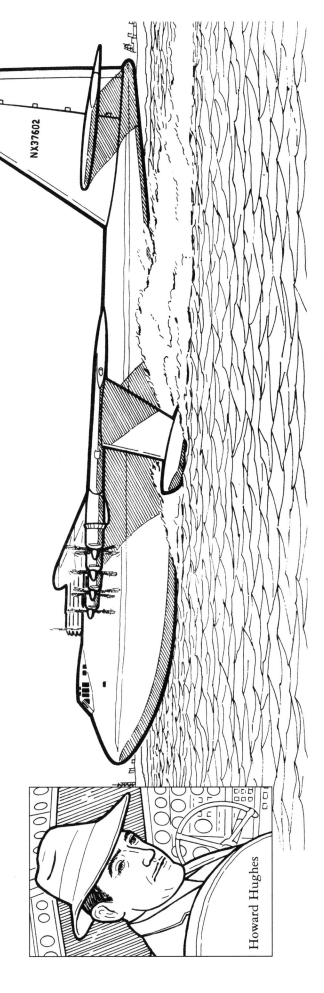

NX37602

Howard Hughes

HUGHES HK-1 (H-4) "HERCULES," 1947

Howard Hughes' most famous aircraft project was the immense flying-boat cargo transport, the HK-1, also designated the H-4. This remarkable airplane is more commonly known, however, as the "Spruce Goose" (although it was constructed largely of birch). The HK-1 project started in World War II as a joint venture between Hughes Aircraft and industrial magnate, Henry J. Kaiser. The purpose of this huge airborne boat—the largest of its kind ever constructed—was to be able to fly hundreds of troops, tanks, artillery, and other needed war materiel from the United States to Europe, thus bypassing the deadly threat posed by German submarines that were then sinking the Allies' merchant ships by the hundreds.

The HK-1 used a flying-boat fuselage, allowing it to take off and land at European ports controlled by the Allies. Everything about the HK-1 was massive. The fuselage itself was 218 feet long, almost three times the length of the World War II Boeing B-17 heavy bomber, with a wingspan ever more colossal—a world-record length of 319 feet from tip to tip. Its huge vertical tail reached fifty feet in height, and even the horizontal tail span of 113 feet was longer than a World War II bomber's main wingspan. To power this 200-ton behemoth, Hughes mounted eight Pratt & Whitney 3,000-horsepower radial engines on the wings. These were the largest and most powerful aircraft piston engines ever

developed, each turning four-bladed propellers seventeen feet in length. The intended range and speed of the HK-1 was 3,000 miles while flying at 200 miles per hour.

Development of the HK-1, which began in 1942, was not fully realized as a single flying prototype airplane until 1947. On November 2, 1947 at 1:40 P.M., Howard Hughes himself piloted the enormous flying boat, lifting off the surface of the Long Beach, California harbor for a brief sixty seconds. He reached an altitude of just seventy feet flying at a speed of ninety miles per hour, covering just over a mile before setting back down onto the ocean. This was the one and only test flight of the "Spruce Goose."

Ironically, by the time the HK-1 was completed, it was already obsolete: the war had ended, flying boats were no longer considered practical, and drastic cutbacks in post-war military spending all served to kill the project. The HK-1 was mothballed and preserved in a hangar for the next thirty-three years. It is currently on exhibit in Long Beach as an unusual piece of aviation history. The HK-1's creator—Howard Hughes—once a brilliant aircraft designer, pilot, and billionaire industrialist, eventually died as an eccentric, paranoid, and obsessive recluse in a Las Vegas hotel room.

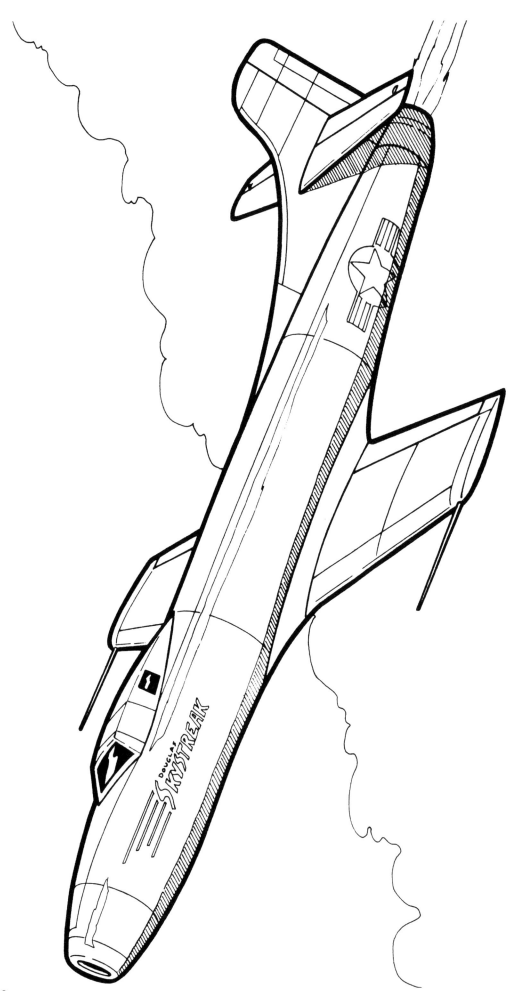

DOUGLAS D-558-1 "SKYSTREAK," 1947

In 1947, Douglas Aircraft designed and built three high-speed research aircraft prototypes for the U.S. Navy, which were intended to explore jet flight characteristics at or near the speed of sound—approximately 715 miles per hour. Flown at Muroc Flight Test Center, the number one D-558-1 Skystreak immediately established world speed records for jet aircraft. On August 20, 1947, test pilot Navy Commander Turner Caldwell reached a speed of 641 miles per hour. Five days later, Marine Major Marion Carl flew the Skystreak to 650 miles per hour. The bright orange test aircraft was 36 feet long, had a wingspan of twenty-five feet, and weighed 10,000 pounds. It was powered by a single Allison J-35 turbojet engine developing 5,000 pounds of thrust. Although one of the Skystreak models was destroyed during testing in 1948, the remaining two are preserved and on exhibit at American naval aviation museums.

BELL X-1, 1947

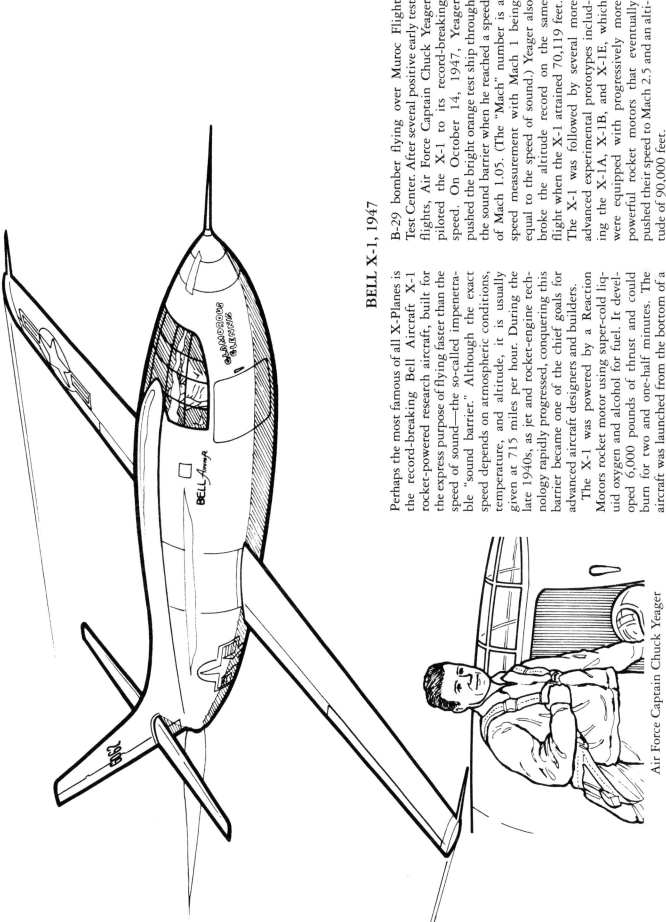

Air Force Captain Chuck Yeager

Perhaps the most famous of all X-Planes is the record-breaking Bell Aircraft X-1 rocket-powered research aircraft, built for the express purpose of flying faster than the speed of sound—the so-called impenetrable "sound barrier." Although the exact speed depends on atmospheric conditions, temperature, and altitude, it is usually given at 715 miles per hour. During the late 1940s, as jet and rocket-engine technology rapidly progressed, conquering this barrier became one of the chief goals for advanced aircraft designers and builders.

The X-1 was powered by a Reaction Motors rocket motor using super-cold liquid oxygen and alcohol for fuel. It developed 6,000 pounds of thrust and could burn for two and one-half minutes. The aircraft was launched from the bottom of a

B-29 bomber flying over Muroc Flight Test Center. After several positive early test flights, Air Force Captain Chuck Yeager piloted the X-1 to its record-breaking speed. On October 14, 1947, Yeager pushed the bright orange test ship through the sound barrier when he reached a speed of Mach 1.05. (The "Mach" number is a speed measurement with Mach 1 being equal to the speed of sound.) Yeager also broke the altitude record on the same flight when the X-1 attained 70,119 feet. The X-1 was followed by several more advanced experimental prototypes including the X-1A, X-1B, and X-1E, which were equipped with progressively more powerful rocket motors that eventually pushed their speed to Mach 2.5 and an altitude of 90,000 feet.

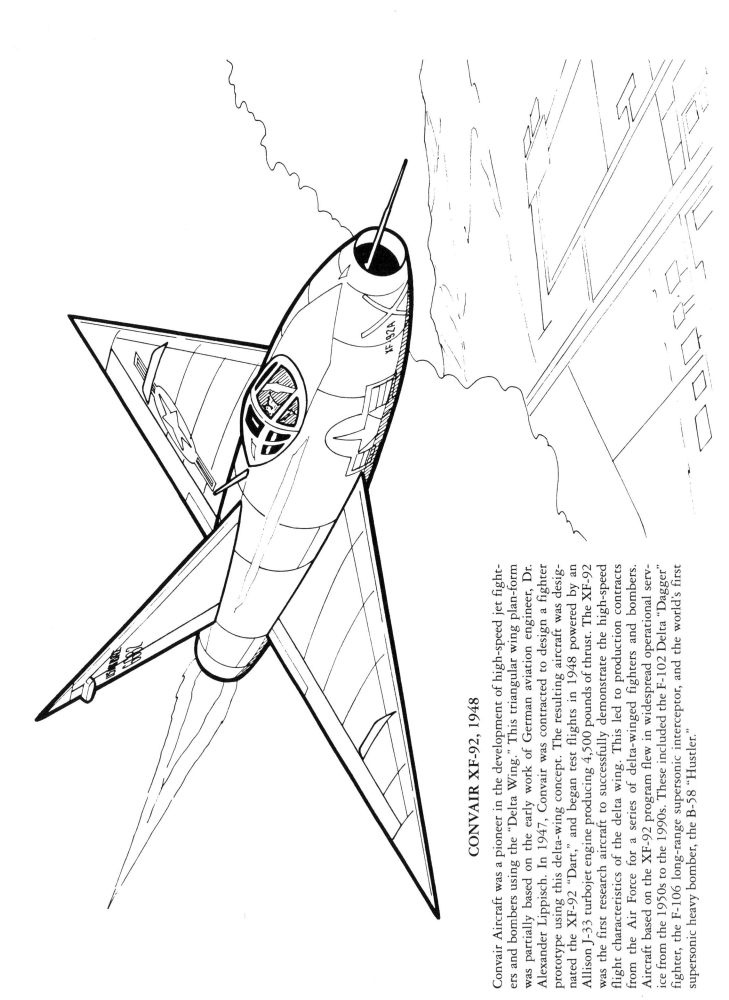

CONVAIR XF-92, 1948

Convair Aircraft was a pioneer in the development of high-speed jet fighters and bombers using the "Delta Wing." This triangular wing plan-form was partially based on the early work of German aviation engineer, Dr. Alexander Lippisch. In 1947, Convair was contracted to design a fighter prototype using this delta-wing concept. The resulting aircraft was designated the XF-92 "Dart," and began test flights in 1948 powered by an Allison J-33 turbojet engine producing 4,500 pounds of thrust. The XF-92 was the first research aircraft to successfully demonstrate the high-speed flight characteristics of the delta wing. This led to production contracts from the Air Force for a series of delta-winged fighters and bombers. Aircraft based on the XF-92 program flew in widespread operational service from the 1950s to the 1990s. These included the F-102 Delta "Dagger" fighter, the F-106 long-range supersonic interceptor, and the world's first supersonic heavy bomber, the B-58 "Hustler."

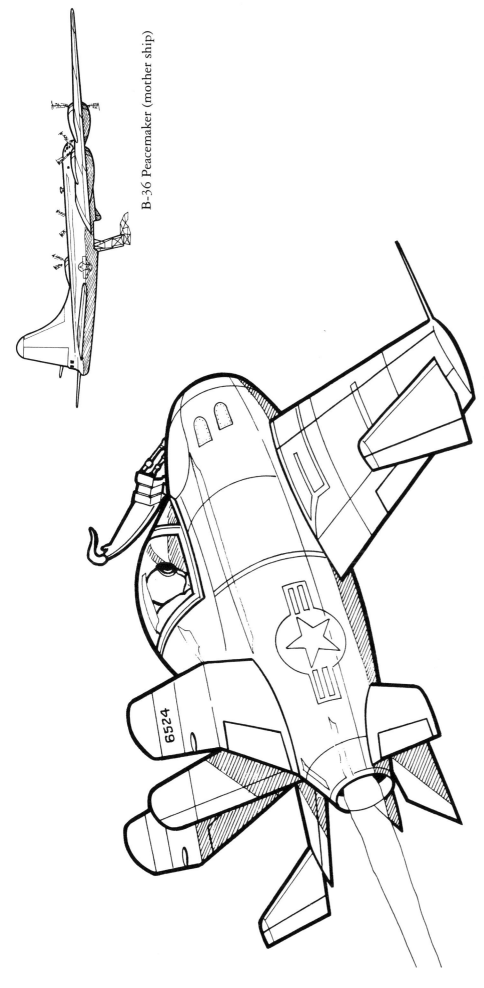

B-36 Peacemaker (mother ship)

McDONNELL XF-85 "GOBLIN," 1948

During the late 1940s and early 1950s, the U.S. Air Force Strategic Air Command (SAC), operated a sizeable fleet of very large intercontinental heavy bombers, the B-36 "Peacemakers." The B-36 was an immense aircraft capable of delivering 72,000 pounds of bombs, including nuclear weapons, over a range of 10,000 miles. Although the B-36 was powered by six propeller engines and four jet engines, it could attain a maximum speed of just over 400 miles per hour. This left the huge bomber vulnerable to enemy jet fighters capable of flying in the 500–600 miles per hour range. In an attempt to protect the B-36, a very small experimental "parasite" fighter prototype was built and rest flown in 1948. The XF-85 Goblin was mounted under the B-36 on a special "trapeze" mechanism intended to enable the XF-85 to be launched, engage enemy fighters, and reconnect to the mother ship.

The diminutive fighter was basically a jet engine with small wings, and several tails and fins, only fifteen feet long with a wingspan of twenty-two feet. Its Westinghouse J-34 turbojet engine could propel the 4,500-pound aircraft at a relatively fast speed of 660 miles per hour. Its small size dictated that it would have just enough fuel for thirty minutes of flight time. It was to be armed with four fuselage-mounted .50-caliber machine guns, and was fitted with a multitude of tail fins and wing tip fins to stabilize its flying characteristics. Even with these numerous flight control surfaces, the inherently poor aerodynamics of the Goblin could not be overcome. The project was cancelled because of these stability problems, as well as the fact that all jet-powered bombers would soon fly fast enough to negate the need for a "parasite" escort fighter.

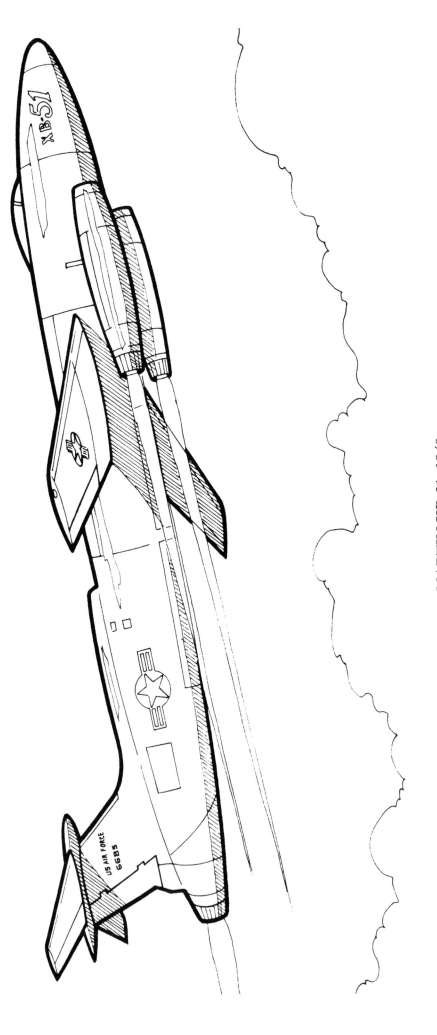

MARTIN XB-51, 1949

An unusual three-engined jet attack bomber concept was developed by Martin Aircraft in 1949. Two flying prototypes of the XB-51 were built and test flown from 1949 to 1952, with the intention of producing a high-speed attack bomber capable of destroying ground targets with both bombs and gunfire. To this end, the XB-51 was fitted with a battery of eight nose-mounted 20-millimeter cannons and a 10,000-pound bomb-load capacity.

The XB-51 featured three General Electric J-47 turbojets: two were externally mounted on the forward fuselage, and one was internally positioned within the rear fuselage. Each developed 5,200 pounds of thrust which gave the XB-51 an impressive top speed of 645 miles per hour. The airplane was fairly large, with a fifty-three foot wingspan and a length of eighty-five feet. Fully loaded, the XB-51 weighed 56,000 pounds. One innovative feature of the aircraft was the internal rotary bomb rack devised to facilitate bomb release while flying at high speed, which was later incorporated into several operational bombers including the B-57, B-1B "Lancer," and B-2 "Spirit" stealth bomber. The XB-51 never made it into production because it was superseded by the Boeing B-47 "Stratojet."

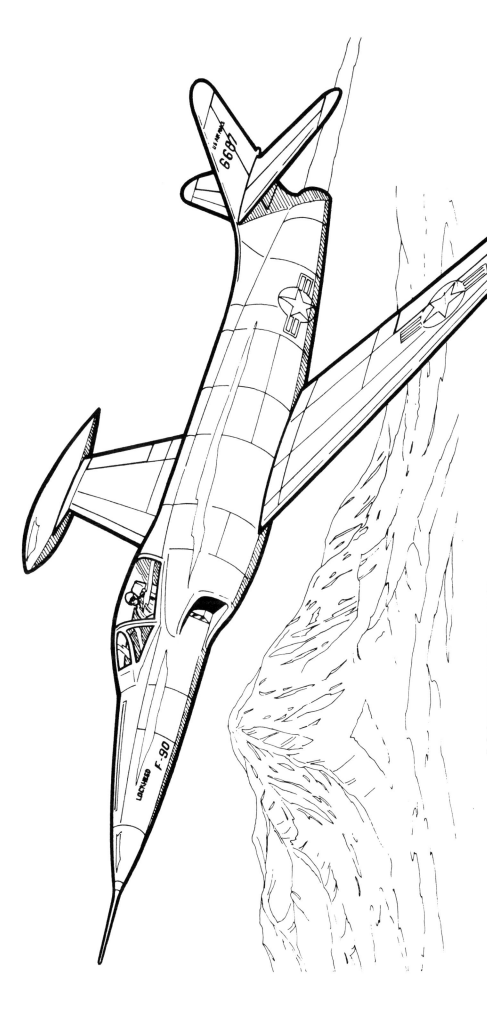

LOCKHEED XF-90, 1949

By the end of the 1940s, the Air Force asked several aircraft companies to design and build prototypes for a high speed, long-range fighter-interceptor, an aircraft type that was needed to counter the ongoing fear among U.S. military planners of invading Russian nuclear bomber fleets during the Cold War years. Long-range interceptors could fly out, then meet and destroy these attacking bombers far from the continental United States.

Three companies competed for this aircraft contract: North American Aviation produced the XF-93, McDonnell the XF-88, and Lockheed created ed the elegant XF-90 pictured above. The Lockheed entry was powered by two Westinghouse J-34 turbojets each producing 4,200 pounds of thrust, which gave the needle-nosed interceptor a top speed of 668 miles per hour in level flight and 739 miles per hour in a dive. The XF-90 was fifty-six feet long and had swept-back wings with a span of forty feet—including the teardrop-shaped wing tip fuel tanks. Although the XF-90 was not chosen by the Air Force—losing out to McDonnell's XF-88—it is considered one of the most beautiful aircraft shapes ever devised.

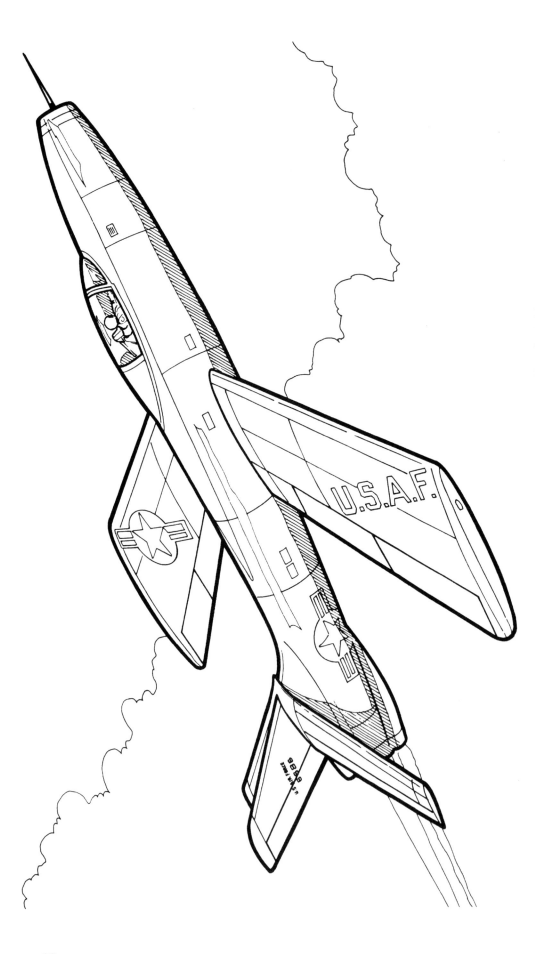

REPUBLIC XF-91 "THUNDERCEPTOR," 1952

A unique hybrid fighter, the XF-91 Thunderceptor, was developed by Republic Aviation beginning in 1949, and was a modification of Republic's existing F-84F "Thunderstreak" jet fighter. The aircraft was powered by both a turbojet engine and a rocket engine, infusing it with both blazing speed potential and a very fast rate of climb (19,000 feet per minute) for its intended role as a bomber-interceptor. The XF-91 was equipped with a General Electric J-34 turbojet producing 5,000 pounds of thrust, and a Reaction Motors rocket engine developing 6,000 pounds of thrust. The rocket exhaust nozzle was located under the jet pipe at the rear of the aircraft's fuselage.

The Thunderceptor also featured an unusual wing design with the width of the wing increasing towards the wing tip, in contrast to the conventional wing shape that is wider at the fuselage mating point than at the wing tip. This innovation was the idea of Republic's famed aircraft designer, Alexander Karrveli, and its purpose was to provide greater lift while permitting high-speed flight and lower landing speeds. With test flights beginning in 1952, the XF-91's two power plants gave the Thunderceptor a supersonic top speed of 1,125 miles per hour. However, problems with both high-speed stability and the rocket engine itself caused the cancellation of the project in 1954.

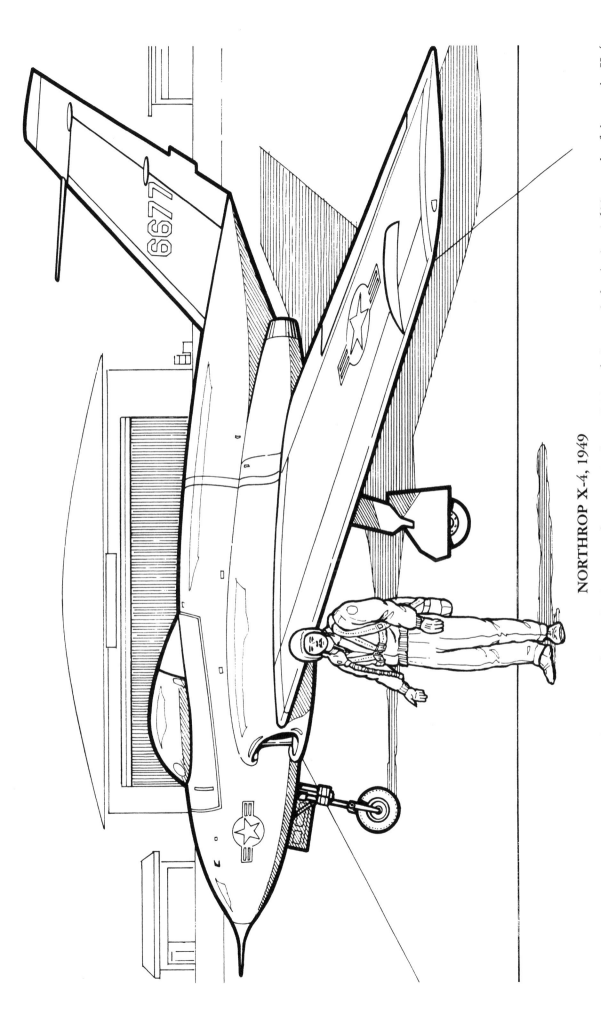

NORTHROP X-4, 1949

The X-4 research jet aircraft illustrated above was a further development of Northrop's flying-wing concept. Its swept-back wings extended almost the full length of the small fuselage, and unlike most other flying-wing aircraft, the X-4 had a large vertical fin-rudder for stability. The aircraft was the smallest X-Plane created with a wingspan of just twenty-six feet and a length of twenty-three feet, and nicknamed the "Bantam" due to its diminutive size. Powered by two

Westinghouse J-30 turbojets, each developing 1,600 pounds of thrust, the X-4 was designed to explore flight characteristics of its wing design at speeds close to the sound barrier (Mach 1). Flight tests of the two X-4 models continued from 1949 to 1954. The airframe was constructed of strong but lightweight magnesium-aluminum alloy, and like many of the X-Planes tested at Edwards Air Force base, the X-4 was painted in a high gloss white finish.

BELL X-5, 1951

Pictured above is the Bell X-5, a unique research prototype designed with swept-back wings that could change their angle of sweep while in flight, pivoting from a mild twenty degrees for low speed flight and landing, to a drastic sixty degrees for high-speed runs—the first aircraft to incorporate this unique capability. Variable sweep wings would later be utilized in several aircraft deployed into widespread service, including the F-14 "Tomcat" Navy fighter, the F-111

"Aardvark" fighter-bomber, and the B1-B Lancer heavy bomber. The X-5 was powered by an Allison J-35 turbojet producing 4,900 pounds of thrust. With a barrel-like fuselage enclosing the engine, the jet exhaust exited from under the upswept tail assembly. The X-5 flights provided important test data for the NACA (National Advisory Council on Aeronautics) research agency, the predecessor of NASA (National Aeronautics and Space Administration).

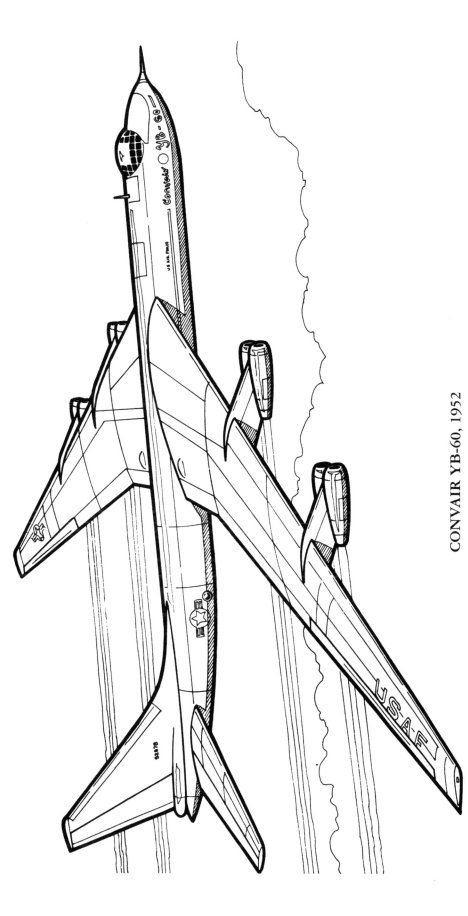

CONVAIR YB-60, 1952

As early as 1946, the U.S. Air Force had issued design requirements for a large, fast bomber able to carry a heavy bomb-load of nuclear weapons over intercontinental distances. The two aircraft companies that took up this challenge with actual flying prototypes were Boeing and Convair. The winner was the entry from Boeing—its famous B-52 "Stratofortress"—considered by many aviation historians to be one of the greatest aircraft ever produced. Nonetheless, the Convair entry was a very close first runner-up.

The Convair YB-60 shown above was a direct descendant of that company's very successful B-36 heavy bomber. The B-36 Peacemaker was widely deployed by the Strategic Air command in the late 1940s and early 50s as the heart of the American nuclear bomber fleet. However, a faster version was needed. The YB-60 used a stretched B-36 fuselage combined with newly designed swept-back wings and tail assembly. Instead of the piston-engine/jet-engine mix of the B-36, the YB-60 was all jet-powered, featuring eight Pratt & Whitney J-57 turbojets with 7,500 pounds of thrust each, mounted in pairs on forward swept pylons located under the wings. It was an immense aircraft, the largest of its day, with a fuselage length of 171 feet, and an enormous wingspan of 206 feet—even larger than the Boeing competitor, the XB-52. The YB-60 could carry a 10,000-pound bomb-load over a distance of 6,500 miles, while cruising at 468 miles per hour; maximum speed was an impressive 508 miles per hour. With a reduced fuel load for less range, the YB-60's bomb-load could be increased to a tremendous 72,000 pounds.

The deciding factor in the Air Force decision to award the production contract to Boeing was the speed differential. The XB-52 had a gross weight of 390,000 pounds, 20,000 pounds lighter than the YB-60, which gave the B-52 the critical edge with a cruising speed of 520 miles per hour and a top speed of 595 miles per hour. The B-52 would go on to serve in the SAC arsenal from 1955 to the present day. Plans call for the latest version—the "H" model—to be continually upgraded in order to serve another twenty-five years, which would give the B-52 a remarkable operational service history of *seventy years!*

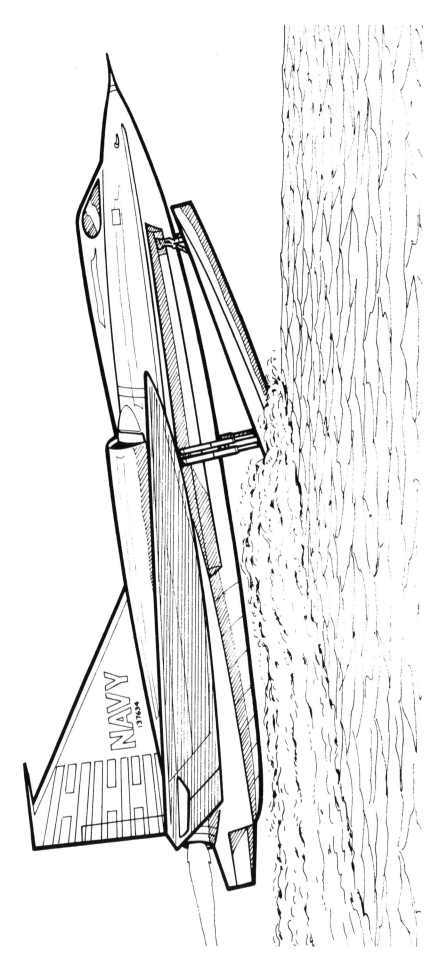

CONVAIR XF2Y-1 "SEA DART," 1953

During the 1950s, Convair developed the technology of the delta wing plan-form with greater success than any other aircraft company. Their series of operational Air Force fighters and bombers were all based on Convair's original delta-wing research prototype, the XF-92 "Dart." A unique experimental aircraft that used the Convair delta-wing concept was the XF2Y-1 Sea Dart, developed for the U.S. Navy as a water-launched jet fighter with a flying boat-type fuselage-hull.

The Sea Dart first flew in 1953, demonstrating sea-borne take-offs and landings. Two different "hydro-ski" landing gear systems were tested. A single large hydro-plane ski lowered and retracted back into the fuselage was used for the initial flights. To increase stability, a two hydro-ski system was used for subsequent flights. The XF2Y-1 was powered by a Westinghouse J-46 turbojet, with the air intakes mounted high on the upper fuselage. The 5,725 pounds of thrust developed by the engine gave the Sea Dart a top speed of 695 miles per hour. During a shallow dive test flight, the aircraft exceeded the sound barrier, becoming the first seaplane to achieve supersonic speed.

The XF2Y-1 program continued into 1954 with the loss of one of the two prototypes during an airshow demonstration flight. The Navy decided to cancel the project primarily due to the lack of interest in a water-borne fighter jet. The Sea Dart was painted in the standard Navy colors of this era—dark sea blue with white markings. Additionally, the large vertical fin was distinguished by a bright yellow striped pattern.

DOUGLAS D-558-2 "SKYROCKET," 1953

The successor to the jet-powered Douglas D-558-1 Skystreak was the swept-wing D-558-2 Skyrocket, illustrated above. The three prototypes constructed were hybrid-powered aircraft, using a small turbojet for take-offs and a powerful rocket motor for the main speed runs. The jet engine was a Westinghouse J-34 developing 3,000 pounds of thrust, while the Reaction Motors four-nozzle rocket produced 6,000 pounds of thrust. The successful test flight program of the Skyrocket lasted from 1948 until 1953.

The D-558-2 took off using its own turbojet, and was also air-launched from a B-29 mother ship. In November, 1953, a Skyrocket with the turbojet removed to allow for extra fuel, was dropped from its mother ship for a record-breaking flight. Flown by famed test pilot Scott Crossfield, the D-558-2 became the first aircraft to fly at twice the speed of sound (1,325 miles per hour) while reaching a world record altitude of 83,235 feet. Data gathered by the supersonic testing of the D-558-2 prototypes provided crucial information for the development of a generation of supersonic fighter jets that were put into operational service in the 1960s. The beautifully designed, sharp-nosed Skyrocket was painted and polished to a brilliant white gloss finish.

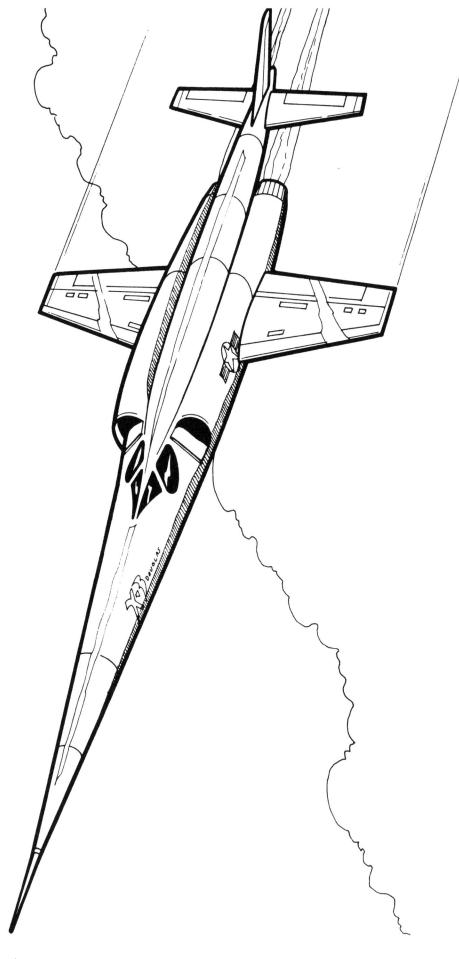

DOUGLAS X-3 "STILETTO," 1953

The needle-nosed Douglas X-3 Stiletto research model shown above looks as if it were traveling at supersonic speed while still parked on the taxi ramp. One of its chief design goals was to investigate heat build-up on the airframe caused by air friction when flying at Mach 2 (twice the speed of sound). The first aircraft to use large amounts of super-strong, heat-resistant titanium for its external skin, the X-3's futuristic appearance was nonetheless belied by its disappointing performance.

The X-3 began test flights in 1953 equipped with two lower-powered Westinghouse J-34 turbojets developing 4,800 pounds of thrust apiece. These engines were eventually to be replaced by more powerful Westinghouse J-46 tur- bojets producing 7,000 pounds of thrust each. Flying with the less potent engines, the X-3 was not even able to reach Mach 1 (700 miles per hour), while development problems with the higher-powered turbojets prevented their instal- lation in the single prototype. Although the Stiletto did not achieve its super- sonic flight potential, the design of its knife-like fuselage and short straight wings was later incorporated into an operational jet fighter. The Lockheed F-104 "Starfighter," one of the fastest of the successful "Century Series" of jet fighters in service from the 1950s to the 1980s, drew directly from the basic airframe design of the X-3.

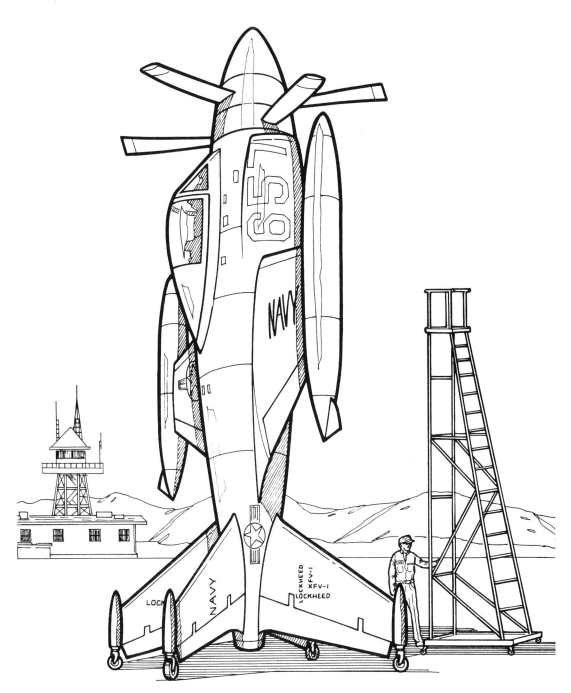

LOCKHEED XFV-1 VERTICAL RISER, 1954

In 1950, the U.S. Navy issued contracts for the development of a ship-borne fighter aircraft that could take off and land vertically. It would be deployed on aircraft carriers, other warships, and even merchant ships, to defend those vessels against enemy aerial attack. Both Lockheed and Convair built flying prototypes for this type of fighter plane, with each of their designs featuring a cruciform (cross-like) "tail-sitter" structure to facilitate vertical take-offs and landings.

Shown above is the Lockheed entry, the XFV-1, nicknamed the "Salmon," primarily in honor of its chief test pilot, Herman "Fish" Salmon, but perhaps also because of its distinctive fish-like shape suggestive of a salmon swimming upstream. Both the Lockheed and Convair models were to be powered by the same engine, a massive Allison T-40 turboprop, which churned out a whopping 5,850 horsepower to turn two sets of paddle-like count-

er-rotating propellers. The estimated top speed was in the 575 to 600 miles per hour range. The Salmon stood thirty-six feet tall with a thirty-foot wingspan. Two large wing tip pods were provided to house 20-millimeter cannons or multiple air-to-air rockets.

During its testing, the XFV-1 never took off vertically, nor did it make the in-flight transition to horizontal flying. Problems with the power output of the Allison turboprop engine prevented this intended function. As a temporary cure, a cumbersome external landing gear assembly was installed to allow the aircraft to take off and land in the conventional horizontal mode. With this system in place, test pilot "Fish" Salmon conducted thirty-two test flights of the XFV-1 during 1954. The unique "tail-sitter" fighter was finished in its natural aluminum, polished to a shiny metallic finish.

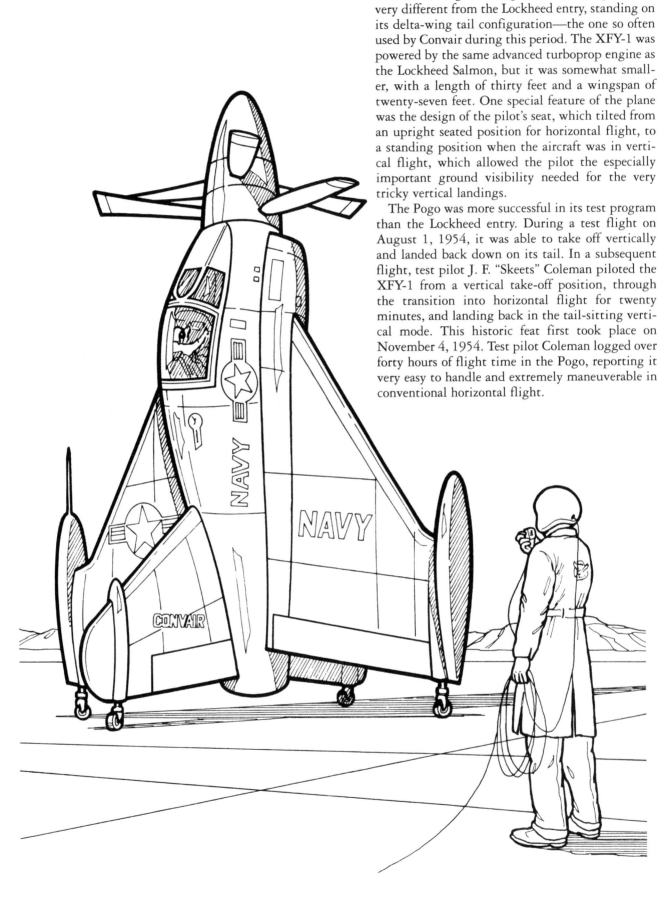

CONVAIR XFY-1 "POGO," 1954

The XFY-1 Pogo was Convair's entry in the Navy's vertical-riser fighter competition. The Pogo looked very different from the Lockheed entry, standing on its delta-wing tail configuration—the one so often used by Convair during this period. The XFY-1 was powered by the same advanced turboprop engine as the Lockheed Salmon, but it was somewhat smaller, with a length of thirty feet and a wingspan of twenty-seven feet. One special feature of the plane was the design of the pilot's seat, which tilted from an upright seated position for horizontal flight, to a standing position when the aircraft was in vertical flight, which allowed the pilot the especially important ground visibility needed for the very tricky vertical landings.

The Pogo was more successful in its test program than the Lockheed entry. During a test flight on August 1, 1954, it was able to take off vertically and landed back down on its tail. In a subsequent flight, test pilot J. F. "Skeets" Coleman piloted the XFY-1 from a vertical take-off position, through the transition into horizontal flight for twenty minutes, and landing back in the tail-sitting vertical mode. This historic feat first took place on November 4, 1954. Test pilot Coleman logged over forty hours of flight time in the Pogo, reporting it very easy to handle and extremely maneuverable in conventional horizontal flight.

RYAN X-13 "VERTIJET," 1955

Since the advent of naval aviation in the early years of the twentieth century, there has been a friendly rivalry between the Navy and the Air Force to develop the most advanced aircraft. The Navy's vertical take-off and landing (VTOL) fighter program inspired a similar effort within the Air Force.

In 1955, Ryan Aircraft built and tested an all-jet powered VTOL prototype for the Air Force. Designated the X-13 Vertijet, the aircraft used a lightweight but powerful Rolls Royce Avon turbojet developing 10,000 pounds of thrust. The engine exhaust nozzle featured a moderate ability to swivel its direction of thrust to regulate stability. Engine exhaust was also directed to small wing tip nozzles to aid vertical flight control. For its initial test, the X-13 was fitted with externally mounted landing

gear that was removable. Subsequently, the aircraft was tested as designed: to take off and land while suspended from a large trapeze bar and hook assembly. The bar extended horizontally between vertical arms of a mobile trailer that could be raised and lowered from a horizontal to a vertical position. The Vertijet was equipped with a hook mounted under the fuselage nose for attaching to the bar.

The X-13 successfully made the transition from vertical to horizontal flight over a series of tests made during 1955. Shown above, the Vertijet is maneuvering toward the hanging trapeze bar with a striped "feeler" pole extended to help guide the pilot. Like the Navy, the Air Force also cancelled its "tail-sitter" program due to changing aircraft requirements.

MARTIN XP6M-1 "SEAMASTER," 1955

Martin Aviation created the ultimate expression of the flying boat seaplane with its multi-jet powered attack airplane, the XP6M-1 Seamaster, first flown in 1955. Designed for the U.S. Navy as a patrol bomber, mine-layer, and high-speed reconnaissance aircraft, the Seamaster was able to reach fighter-like speeds of 600 miles per hour despite its large size. The XP6M-1 featured sharply swept-back wings spanning 100 feet, and a fuselage length of 120 feet. Its Allison J-71 turbojet engines were mounted on top of the wing to avoid water intake. The plane

was designed to fly over the open ocean for long periods of time at altitudes as high as 50,000 feet. With its distinctly designed fuselage-hull and wing-tip floats, the XP6M-1 could take off and land in fairly choppy seas. Martin Aviation produced a number of successful flying boats that were deployed into operational service, including the World War II PBM Mariner, the post-war P5M Marlin, and the giant JRM Mars transport.

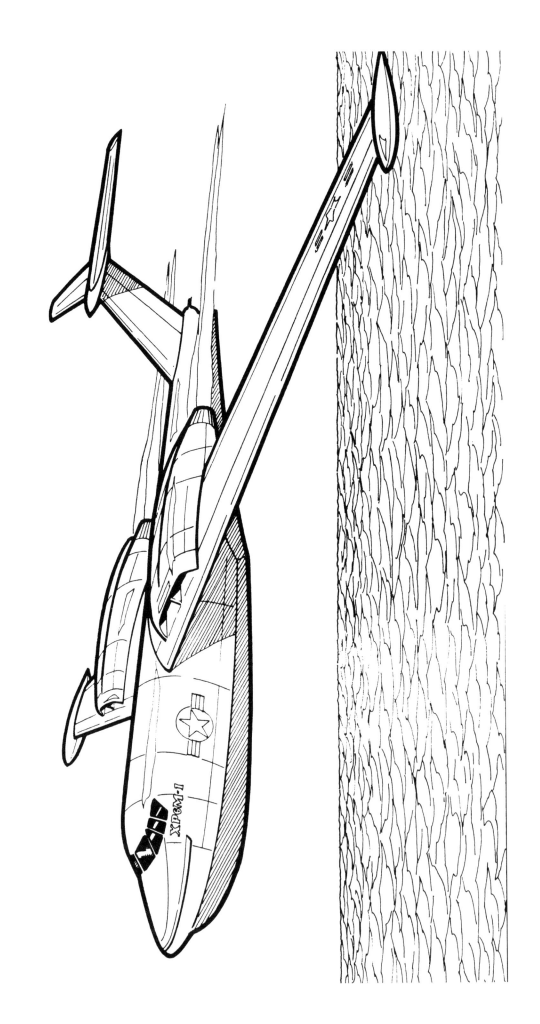

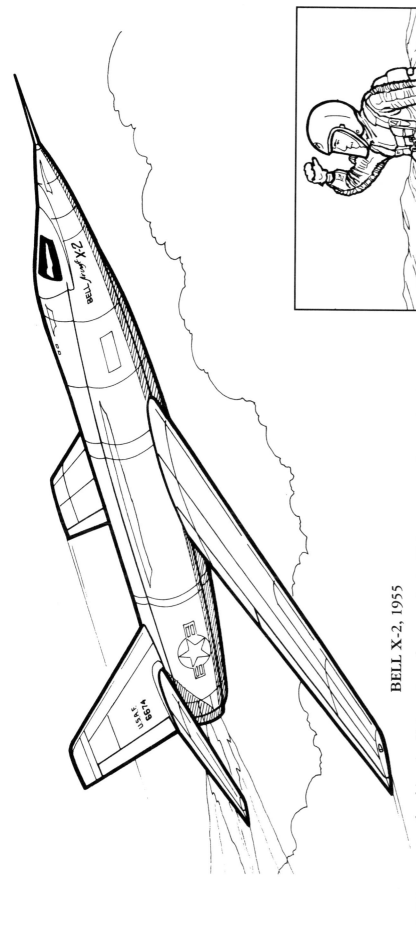

Test Pilot in
1950s–60s "G" Suit

BELL X-2, 1955

The successor to the historic X-1 series of rocket-powered research aircraft was the swept-wing X-2, designed to fly at three times the speed of sound (2,100 miles per hour). It was also intended to explore the use of high-strength stainless steel fuselage skin to deal with the very high temperature range created by its supersonic flight. The X-2 proved to be a difficult aircraft to fly at such extreme speeds.

The X-2's first rocket-powered flight occurred in November, 1955 with test pilot Pete Everest at the controls. In July, 1956, Air Force Captain Iven Kinchloe piloted the X-2 to a record-breaking speed of Mach 2.93 and an altitude of 126,600 feet. On September 7, 1956, the X-2 made its final flight, when test pilot Milburn "Mel" Apt pushed the aircraft to another record speed of 2,094 miles per hour, three times the speed of sound. At that

speed, the X-2 went out of control and crashed, killing Mel Apt.

Pictured above, the beautiful white X-2 with its sharply swept wings and needle nose, was powered by a Curtiss-Wright XLR25 rocket motor generating a tremendous thrust of 15,000 pounds. Inset is a test pilot in a 1950s–60s "G" suit, an outfit specially designed to counteract the negative effects of increased gravity on the human body caused by the high acceleration and rapid maneuvering inherent in rocket-powered flight. Although the X-2 proved to be a dangerous, even deadly X-Plane, the data gathered by its testing was instrumental in developing the most successful X-Plane ever flown, the North American X-15.

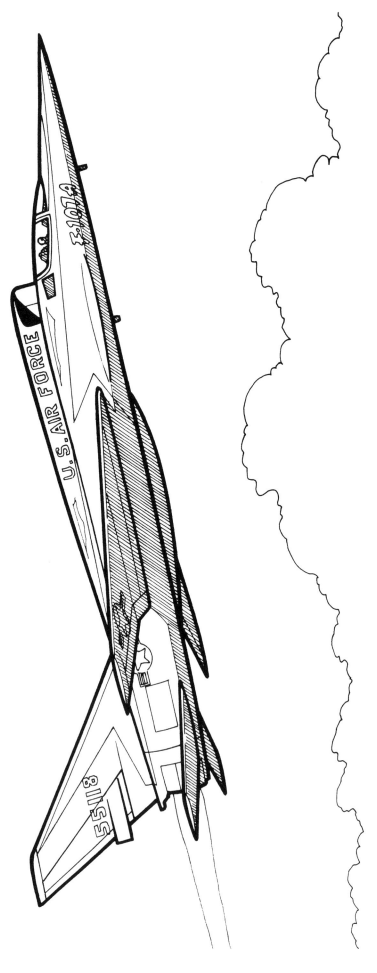

NORTH AMERICAN YF-107 "ULTRA SABRE," 1956

During World War II, North American Aviation grew from a second-tier aircraft company to a leader in advanced airplane design. Its B-25 Mitchell medium bomber and its P-51 Mustang fighter were highly successful and effective aircraft. The Mustang is considered by many pilots and aviation historians to be the best propeller-driven fighter ever built. After World War II, North American produced America's first swept-wing jet fighter, the famous F-86 Sabre Jet. During the Korean War, Sabre jets flew in combat and defeated enemy MIG-15 jet fighters with a kill-ratio of seventeen to one.

In the early 1950s, North American designed and built the first supersonic jet fighter to go into widespread service. The initial entry into the "Century Series" of jet fighters, the F-100 "Super Sabre" could reach a speed of 825 miles per hour in level flight. It went on to become a workhorse fighter-bomber during the Vietnam War (1964–1973). The North American YF-107 Ultra Sabre prototype pictured above began as an improved model of the F-100, but eventually became a completely separate aircraft program. Designed for speeds higher than the

F-100, the YF-107 was powered by a Pratt & Whitney J-79 turbojet engine developing a tremendous thrust of 24,500 pounds. In its test flights beginning in 1956, the YF-107 was able to reach an impressive top speed of 1,541 miles per hour. One of the aircraft's most unique features was the jet engine air intake that was mounted on top of the fuselage behind the pilot canopy.

The YF-107 was designed for the dual role of air superiority fighter and fighter-bomber, to compete for a production contract against the McDonnell F-101 "Voodoo," already chosen for production, and the Republic YF-105 "Thunderchief," which was undergoing flight testing similar to the YF-107. In 1957, the F-107 program was cancelled by the Air Force after they selected the Republic F-105 for their advanced fighter-bomber. Because of the YF-107's very high speed, however, two of the three Ultra Sabre prototypes continued to fly for several more years. They were used by NASA at the Edwards Air Force Base Flight Test Center to explore aerodynamics and maneuverability at supersonic speeds.

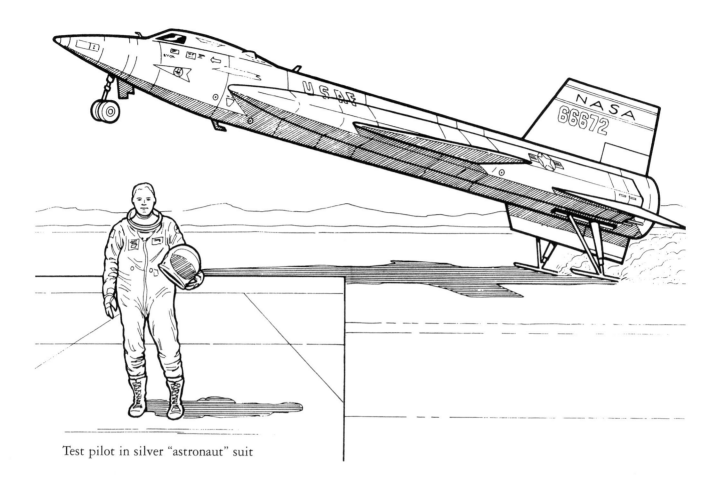

Test pilot in silver "astronaut" suit

NORTH AMERICAN X-15, 1959

The X-15 rocket plane flew higher and faster than any aircraft in existence during its test flight program that lasted from 1959 to 1968. It still holds world speed and altitude records for manned aircraft. Three X-15's were built and flown during their nine-year service lives, and they made a total of 199 test flights.

The X-15's were built by North American Aviation to be powered by a Reaction Motors–Thikol XLR99-RM-2 rocket motor generating 58,000 pounds of thrust. The aircraft were fifty feet long and had short straight wings with a span of twenty-two feet, with both a top and bottom tail fin at the rear of the fuselage. The X-15's were air-launched from a B-52 mother ship at altitudes over 35,000 feet. After making their high-speed runs and exhausting the fuel supply, the aircraft glided to a touchdown on rear-landing gear skids and a front nose wheel. The lower tail fin was jettisoned before landing.

One of the first world records set by an X-15 took place in 1961 when test pilot Bob White flew the aircraft at the speed of Mach 6, over 4,000 miles per hour. In 1962, pilot White took the X-15 to a world record altitude of 314,750 feet, over sixty miles high. Since outer space is officially considered to start at fifty miles up, the X-15 became a spacecraft as well as an aircraft. For this achieve-

ment, Bob White was awarded his "astronaut wings." During the years of the X-15 test flight program, a total of eight pilots guided the three aircraft past the fifty-mile limit, entitling them to astronaut status.

In 1963, one of the X-15's was rebuilt to incorporate a longer fuselage and large external fuel tanks. This extra fuel increased the rocket motor's burn time by seventy percent. The standard black paint finish was also changed to a heat-resistant white. On October 3, 1967, this model of the aircraft, the X-15A-2, was flown by Air Force pilot William "Pete" Knight to its fastest speed, an unofficial world record of 4,523 miles per hour. Shortly after that, test pilot Mike Adams was killed in a crash of one of the other X-15's. It was the only fatality during nine years of testing and 199 flights.

On October 28, 1968, chief test pilot Bill Dana took the X-15 on its last historic flight. The two remaining X-15's were retired and are now on exhibit at the National Air and Space Museum in Washington, D.C., and the Air Force Museum in Dayton, Ohio. The research data gathered by these remarkable X-Planes was crucial in the design and development of America's next space plane—the Space Shuttle.

NORTH AMERICAN XB-70 "VALKYRIE," 1964

The elegant and futuristic-looking bomber prototype depicted above was one of two XB-70 Valkyrie aircraft that were designed and built by North American Aviation. Developed as "triple-sonic" intercontinental bombers, they were intended to deliver nuclear weapons over enemy territory from extreme altitudes. The test flight program of the two prototypes lasted from 1964 to 1969.

The XB-70 was a massive aircraft, in terms of both size and performance. The plane's enormous fuselage stretched 185 feet from twin tails to a slender snake-like nose. It was designed with huge delta wings spanning 105 feet, which incorporated wing tips that folded down to a maximum angle of sixty-five degrees to aid in ultrasonic flight. The power plants for this super-bomber were the most advanced turbojets of the day, with six General Electric YJ93 engines arranged in a horizontal row across the tail of the aircraft. Each engine generated a tremendous 31,000 pounds of thrust. With its impressive cruise speed of 2,000 miles per hour at an altitude of 70,000 feet, the XB-70's mission

was to penetrate Soviet airspace by out-racing enemy fighter or missile defenses.

On April 8, 1966, test pilots Fitzhugh "Fitz" Fulton and Al White demonstrated the XB-70's intended flight performance when they cruised for sixteen minutes at Mach 3.07, at an altitude of 73,000 feet. Shortly after this record-breaking flight, the second XB-70 prototype collided with an F-104 chase plane while flying in formation. The mid-air collision resulted in the crash of both aircraft and the death of their pilots. The B-70 program was cancelled in 1969. Advances in Soviet air defense, as well as politically-based funding difficulties in Congress, killed further development of this remarkably fast and high-flying aircraft. The one remaining XB-70 is now on permanent exhibit at the Air Force Museum in Dayton, Ohio.

GRUMMAN X-29, 1984

A radical concept in jet-fighter design was explored by the Grumman X-29 prototype pictured above. Two were built to investigate a number of advanced ideas, including carbon fiber materials for the airframe construction, triple-redundant fly-by wire electronics, forward canard wings with rear strake flaps and, of course, the unique forward-swept wings. Prior research data had indicated that this wing plan-form could significantly increase aircraft agility and maneuverability, critical characteristics for air-to-air fighter combat.

The X-29 is powered by a single General Electric F404 turbofan jet engine producing 16,000 pounds of thrust. With a wingspan of twenty-seven feet and a length of forty-eight feet, the X-29 could reach a speed of 1,200 miles per hour. The X-29 testing program began in 1984 and continued until 1992. The two prototypes were flown on 302 research flights at Edwards Air Force Base. The data gathered over the eight years of testing proved very valuable in the design of the Advanced Tactical Fighter (ATF), scheduled to enter operational service with the Air Force sometime in the year 2000.

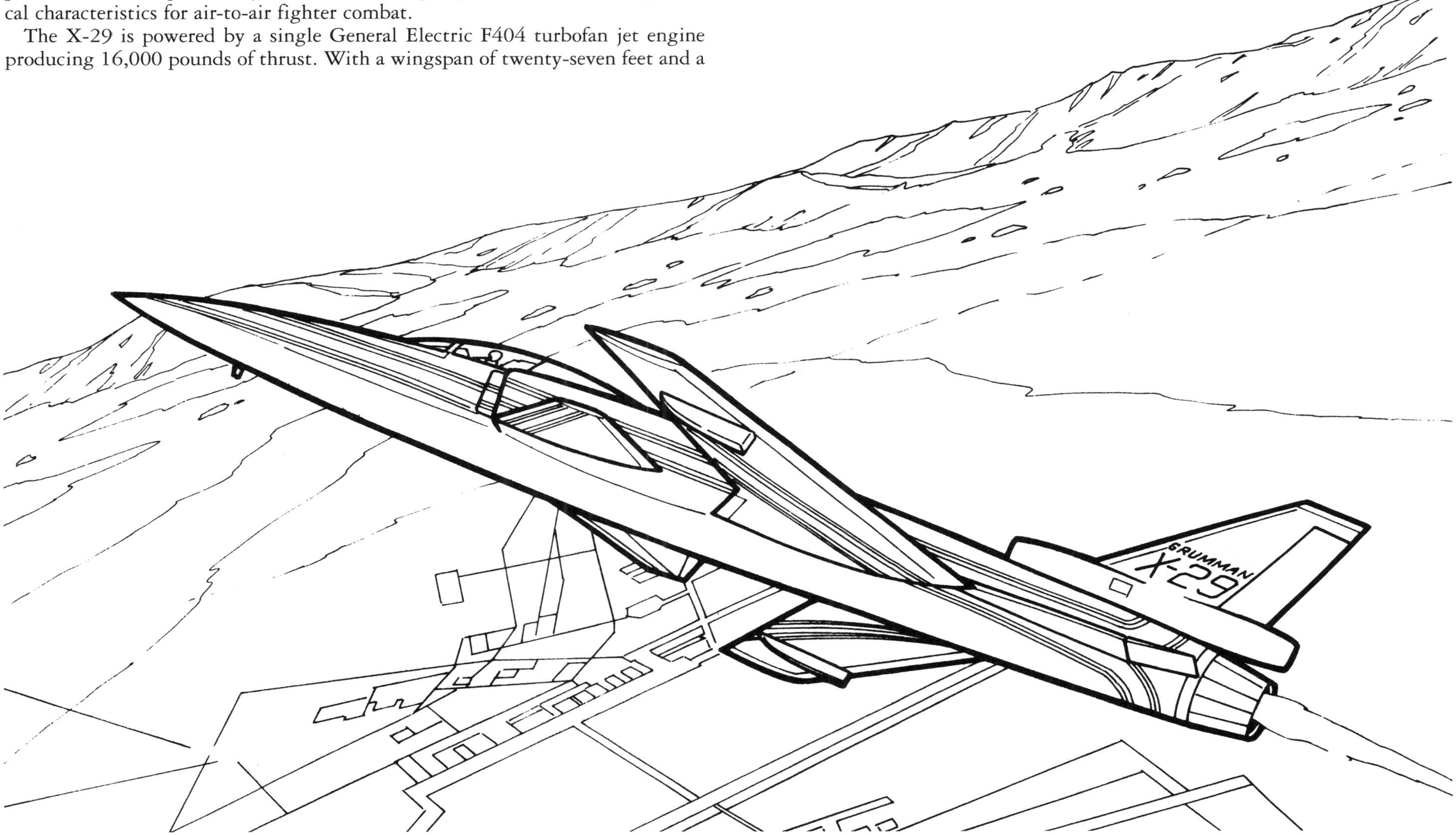

43

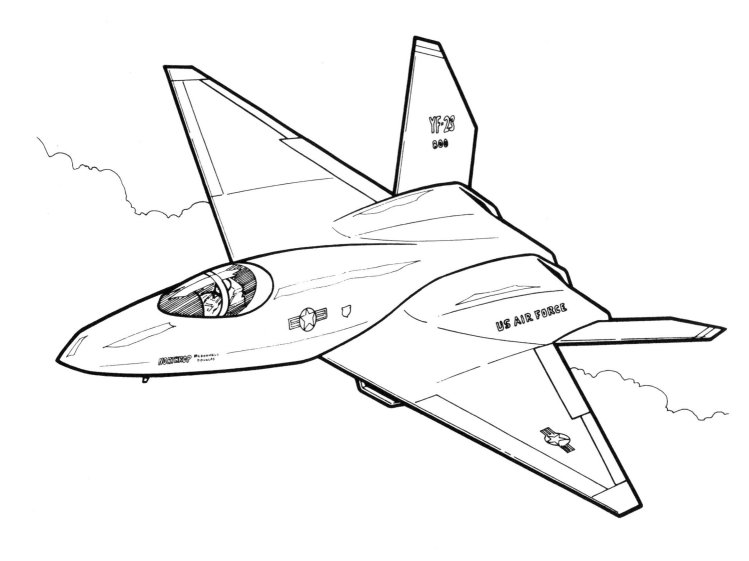

NORTHROP–MCDONNELL DOUGLAS YF-23, 1990

The YF-23 program was part of the Air Force's request for development of an ATF intended for service after the year 2000, replacing both the F-15 "Eagle" and the F-16 "Fighting Falcon" as the premier American fighter aircraft of the 21st century. Two different aviation company conglomerates were in competition for this lucrative Air Force production contract.

Lockheed–Boeing–General Dynamics developed their prototype, the YF-22, to compete in test flight evaluation against the YF-23—the product of a joint venture between Northrop and McDonnell Douglas. Both aircraft were designed to incorporate the three main performance characteristics needed by the Air Force: they were required to cruise at supersonic speeds (at least 1,000 miles per hour) for extended periods of time; provide unprecedented maneuverability; and include radar-evading "stealth" technology. Both competing products fulfilled these criteria with impressive results.

In 1986, design work began on two prototypes of the YF-23, a beautiful but unusually-shaped fighter aircraft, which were ready for for flight testing in July, 1990. The

YF-23, depicted above, was built with both advanced carbon fiber composite and radar-absorbing materials (RAM), featuring a smoothly blended wing-body design with diamond-shaped wings and tail. The plane carried all of its armament within internal bays, including one multi-barrel cannon, four short-range "Sidewinder" missiles, and four AIM-120 medium-range missiles. The YF-23 is powered by two turbofan jet engines developing 35,000 pounds of thrust apiece, giving the sleek fighter a top speed of 1,750 miles per hour (Mach 2.5), and a cruising speed of 1,050 miles per hour (Mach 1.5). The aircraft is sixty-seven feet long with a wingspan of forty-three feet.

The testing program between the competing fighter prototypes lasted until 1991. Although an extremely close contest, the Air Force finally selected the rival YF-22 as the winner of the ATF production contract. Its thrust vectoring exhaust nozzles proved to be the critical factor in the YF-22's greater agility. The two existing YF-23 prototypes have been preserved by Northrop.